UNEXPECTED

The Vault

By:
New York Times, Wall Street Journal, and USA Today
bestselling author
Aleatha Romig

COPYRIGHT AND LICENSE INFORMATION

UNEXPECTED

Paul

What will happen... when Jenn learns the truth that has been
brewing deep inside me?
...when she learns my desires have been restrained?
...when containing them is no longer possible?
Will she flee when there's no place to run?

Traveling to the isolation of a tropical island, we agree to lay our marriage and our future on the line. It's the only way to face the demons—my demons—that threaten our life together.

For us to make our marriage work, we must break down barriers, reveal the hidden places, and shine light where darkness has taken root.

This reprieve from life is meant to be about us, our marriage, and our future.

It is...until the unexpected happens...

Will our marriage survive? Will we?

This suspenseful, steamy stand-alone novella follows Paul and Jenn Masters, characters previously introduced in the novella UNCONVENTIONAL. This quick, spicy story may be read completely on its own or even before UNCONVENTIONAL.

If you enjoy a fast and furious, heart-thundering ride that leaves you breathless and perhaps a bit hot and bothered, check out New York Times bestselling author Aleatha Romig's THE VAULT novellas: UNCONVEN-TIONAL and UNEXPECTED.

Have you been Aleatha'd?

TRIGGER WARNING

This novella explores consensual play in the area of domination and submission. There are also memories and a scene in which those boundaries are tested and crossed. If any of this is a trigger for you, please return this novella and do not read.

However, if you enjoy pushing your boundaries, are curious, and enjoy a lot of heat with an HEA, then please read and enjoy UNEXPECTED.

CHAPTER ONE

Jenn

I bite my lower lip, trying to hold back the tears, as I stare down at the papers before me, wondering how it all came down to this. How can six years of marriage be defined and dissolved in a litany of legal phrases, paragraphs, and division of assets?

"You both need to look at the paperwork carefully," Jonas Miller, our attorney, says. "If everything looks good, all you need to do is sign. Once you both sign, for all practical purposes, it's done." His head bobs in agreement. "We need the judge's signature, but basically, it's all done."

All done.

The phrase rings in my head like bells from an old-time church.

Each clang a memory of happier times past.

Taking a sideways glance at my soon-to-be ex-husband, for some reason, my mind goes back to the afternoon he proposed.

Many of my friends tell stories of how they knew the proposal was coming, how they anticipated and planned. Maybe I'm dense, but when Paul popped the question, for me, it was out of the blue. We'd only been dating for six months, meeting for the first time at a work party. He wasn't a coworker at the firm. He was the friend of a colleague and came along at the last minute. That impulsive decision on his part changed our lives—even if we sign today, that change is forever. From the first moment we met, we hit it off. All I can recall from that party was talking to Paul. The rest of the people ceased to exist. Before we parted ways, he entered his phone number into my phone, and unbeknownst to me, sent himself a text.

We were connected.

It wasn't until the next morning when my phone buzzed that I saw the message he'd sent.

From my phone (the text he sent the night before): *"Hey, it was great meeting you. Let's have lunch tomorrow?"*

From his phone, the next morning: *"I couldn't respond sooner—I was busy thinking about you. Lunch sounds great. I'll pick you up at noon. Address?"*

I had to giggle. It looked like I'd been the one to ask him out, but we both knew the truth. He was both sides of the conversation. Of course, I sent him my address along with a smiling emoji.

I hadn't been looking for forever, so when it found me, I didn't recognize it.

Six months later, the two of us went away for the weekend, up to a secluded resort in northern Wisconsin. There were no fancy restaurants or tall buildings. Instead, we were surrounded by the beauty of nature. For three days we hiked trails and found remote vistas with stunning views. On the final day, we took off early in the morning, walking until we finally made it to the shore of a quiet, out-of-the-way lake. From his backpack Paul pulled out a blanket, a bottle of Champagne, orange juice, and food. He had all the makings of a picnic break-fast, complete with mimosas. Lying on that blanket, staring up at the white fluffy clouds as they floated across the cobalt blue sky, we did what had come naturally to us since the night we first met. We talked.

We shared.

We listened and heard.

As the words on the attorney's papers blur, the heavi-ness in my heart reminds me that somewhere along the way we lost that essential element of our relationship.

Sometime during the last six years while navigating life's ups and downs, we both lost the ability to listen, or perhaps we lost the desire to make time to listen—to make time for one another.

Talking hasn't been an issue. We speak—sometimes obsessively.

We have both been known to say things we regret.

No, talking isn't our issue.

Listening is.

On that afternoon that seems like a lifetime ago, Paul sat up, took my hand, looked into my eyes with his sexy brown-eyed stare, and asked, "Jenn, will you be mine forever?"

As a lump formed in my throat, I found myself lost in his alluring gaze. "Forever?"

"That's a mighty long time..." We both laughed at the reference to lyrics of a song we both enjoyed and could recite in its entirety. He went on. "...but I'm here to tell you—"

"Yes," I said, nodding as I interrupted a classic Prince hit. "It is a long time, and I want to spend it all with you."

"Mrs. Masters," Mr. Miller says, disrupting my thoughts and bringing me back to the present. "Is there a problem with anything in the paperwork?"

"I-I..." I stutter, unable to find the right words. After all we've said and done, I don't know if I can admit that I don't want to sign, that even though I thought I was ready...I'm not. I'm not ready to give up on our forever.

"Jenn?" Paul asks. "We agreed to a no-contest divorce. Everything is divided equally. If you'd feel better with us each having separate representation...?"

I shake my head.

"Is there something you want that isn't listed?" Paul asks. "If you want to keep the house, you can buy me out. When we talked about it, though, you agreed that it would be a lot for you to maintain. Or...the market is good. We should be able to get a decent, if not above-asking price, and then we'll divide the profit down the middle."

"It just seems too final," I finally manage to say as I choke back the emotion and wonder how we got this far.

"It is final," the attorney agrees. "Unless you two need to think about it, but come on... You've both been involved in this marriage. You both agree it's over. You can't expect this to go on forever."

My gaze snaps to our attorney and then immediately to Paul.

Forever.

Forever?

Forever!

As my gaze meets Paul's, more tears sting my eyes, threatening to spill down my cheeks. I search his expression, hoping to see the same emotions I'm feeling. I wish with all my heart he could remember the question he asked me years ago.

I want one more chance.

Silence fills the small conference room.

Loud, thundering silence.

Not even the hum of the air conditioner or the distant tune of the sound system is heard. It's the kind of quiet that echoes in never-ending emptiness. If this were a movie it would be filled with the ticking of a clock, perhaps punctuated by the shrill scream of an alarm. Then again, even TV shows have learned the power of silence. The lack of the show's familiar tune during the credits following the Red Wedding will forever haunt *Game of Thrones* fans.

It's the unpredictability of silence that embodies the fear of the unknown.

What will follow?

The silence surrounding us is as powerful as that used for dramatic effect. It hangs heavily in the air, an unmoving fog clouding our future in a cloak of uncertainty.

Finally, Paul reaches out, covering my hand with his own and stares into my eyes. His warm reassurance is all it takes to break the looming cloud.

I swallow, wondering if I've ever been this scared in my life.

I've been frightened for other reasons, but this is different. This isn't about my physical welfare, but about the loss of something I don't know if I can bear to lose.

I'm not scared to be on my own. I can do it. I've been on my own before. I'm scared to lose the one man whom I truly believed was my forever.

His eyes widen, silently questioning me.

With a quick nod of my head, I let him know that I'm listening.

"Dr. Kizer," he says to me, "recommended that trip. She had a travel agent ready who could book everything."

Dr. Kizer has been our marriage counselor, one recommended by a friend. Unfortunately, our result doesn't seem to be the same as the outcome of our friends. They're off to another state and happily married with a little bundle of joy. We're in an attorney's office about to sign divorce papers.

I swallow again, knowing that the reason my mouth is so damp is due to the tears I'm trying not to shed. "I remember, but we said we couldn't afford it."

Paul tilts his head toward the papers laid out before both of us. "What if we were wrong?"

"About?" I ask.

"About all of it."

"All of it—from the beginning?"

"No, Jenn. We haven't been wrong since the beginning. Two weeks. We call the travel agent Dr. Kizer recommended. We book the trip, and if we're wrong and the marriage is over, when we return home we sign these damn papers." He shrugs his broad shoulders. "If Dr. Kizer is right and we need time alone to really understand one another, then we'll know. No unanswered questions. The worst that can happen is that we spend some of the profit from the house."

"And if she's right and we're not wrong?"

"Then our forever won't be defined in these papers."

The edge of my lip quirks upward. "*Forever?*" I ask. "Do you remember that?"

"I do. I remember too much."

I nod my head, knowing what he means. Along with

the good memories, we have the bad. Is it worth a two-week delay to maybe get nowhere? "Paul, I'm scared."

"Of what?"

"To have hope."

"It's scarier not to have hope. Don't you think?"

For the first time in months, a weight lifts from my chest, and my grin blossoms. With only a few words of his, I remember why I fell in love with this man in the first place. "It feels good to smile."

"It feels good to see you smile."

"After making it this far, this change of plans is..." I search for the right word.

"Unexpected," Mr. Miller volunteers.

I stare into my husband's brown eyes. "Yes. An *unexpected* but hopeful detour."

Paul turns toward our attorney. "We're sorry to have wasted your afternoon. My wife and I aren't ready to sign these papers. Not yet."

Mr. Miller's furrowed brow relaxes as his cheeks also rise. "Listen. I'm a divorce attorney. I'm going to be here in two weeks or a month or whenever you need me or if you don't. This line of work can be a bit disheartening, but if I can offer a bit of advice?"

With my hand in Paul's we both nod.

"You mentioned Dr. Kizer?"

"Yes," I say.

"I presume you mean the marriage counselor?"

Again, we both nod.

"That woman has taken some of my best clients away

from me. She's one of the good ones." He waves his hand. "Don't worry about me. I'm still charging you for drawing up these papers, but filing them, well, my advice is to take this unexpected chance. If it works, Dr. Kizer has done it to me again. If it doesn't, we're prepared. Either way, you'll know."

Paul and I look to one another.

"Two weeks?" he asks.

My mind fills with deadlines and obligations. "I'm involved in a case...I'm not sure I can get away—"

"You can always sign today and move on," Mr. Miller interrupts.

"Jenn?"

I nod my head. "Call the travel agent. Let's leave as soon as possible."

CHAPTER TWO

Paul

Seclusion. Privacy. Time to think, talk, and come to terms.

That's what Dr. Kizer's travel agent promised.

With his help and Dr. Kizer's recommendation, in less than three hours after leaving the attorney's office, Jenn and I were booked on a ten-day getaway to a small northern Belize island. The website boasts turquoise blue water and remote over-water luxury huts.

Apparently, this late in the summer is considered off-season. Because of that, on an island that can house up to three families, we will be the only inhabitants—our own small island in the middle of the Caribbean. While there are two other huts on the island, during our entire stay, we have been promised that they will remain unoccupied.

We're currently flying above the island that will be

our temporary home, and the view is spectacular. The first part of our journey took us to the airport in Belize. We were then picked up by a car service and driven to a small private heliport. The open-sided helicopter affords us a panoramic view of the gorgeous blue Caribbean, dotted with green islands and outlined with white sand, as well as the warmth of the tropical sea breeze.

Jenn squeezes my hand as her face tilts downward, her eyes widening as she takes in the beauty. Her grip intensifies as we begin to descend, coming closer to the ground and sea. With each movement lower, the waves grow from ripples to white caps and the green terrain blossoms to tall trees on hilly terrain.

"Mr. and Mrs. Masters," Miguel, a young man with a Kriol accent, says, speaking through the microphone and headset as he maneuvers the helicopter. "You can see the entire island from up here." He points to a tall wooden tower. "Look to your right. Do you see that flag?"

"Yes," we both say, taking in the green flag flying from the tower.

"There isn't cell service this far out—only satellite or the radio. Each hut has a two-way radio, but if for any reason you need assistance or decide to do an excursion and you can't reach us via the radio, fly a yellow flag. Someone from the resort flies over each island at least three times a day and stops once."

Without saying a word, Jenn's eyes grow even wider as her grip of my hand tightens.

"There is a red flag," Miguel goes on. "Only fly that

for emergencies. Once a day, we'll stop and bring supplies to the central building. Right now, it is equipped with over a week's worth of food, water, and medical supplies. It's not too late to decide to have a chef on the island. After all, besides the center building, there are two empty huts. Someone can stay here with you."

"You're sure there's no one else here?" Jenn asks as she continues to look downward at the island.

"Yes, ma'am. The only way on and off is helicopter or boat. The tides are unpredictable this time of year. Helicopter is the safest. If you decide to do an excursion, we'll fly you to the marina."

"Thank you for the offer," I say. "We decided it would be more fun to just be the two of us. The website said there are grills and other cooking facilities."

"Yes, sir. The freezer is well stocked and there is even fishing equipment available if you want fresh seafood as well as a map to let you know where to fish and swim. Remember, this isn't Disney. The sea creatures are wild. Please heed our safety instructions."

I smile at Jenn. "This will be fun. It'll be like camping."

We both look out to the blue sea that goes on forever, the white sand of the beach, and the tall palm trees making the middle of the island a dense forest of green.

"Like camping in paradise," Jenn says. "With sharks."

"And jellyfish," Miguel offers. "However, stingrays, cone shells, and man-of-war are the biggest concerns in the water. On land, it's spiders and snakes."

"Paul?" My wife's voice sounds uncertain through the earphones.

"Ma'am, your hut is treated against the spiders and ants. Being over the water helps. That's why we constructed them that way. I'm not trying to scare you, only warn you."

"We have spiders and snakes in Wisconsin," I remind my wife.

"Okay," she answers with the same uneasy cadence.

All at once, sand begins to fly as the helicopter descends, the propellers whirling, until the landing blades beneath us settle into the soft sand.

"Stay seat belted until the propellers stop," our guide warns.

Once we're back on solid ground, Miguel unloads our suitcases and bids us to follow along a narrow, well-packed path. Quickly, the elevation increases along with the warm tropical breeze. From the highest elevation we can see out over the sea.

"From the air, you should have seen all three huts at relatively equal distances around the perimeter of the island. This island is our farthest one from the mainland, nearly twenty nautical miles. The closest island to you is over three miles away. During calm seas, that can be reached by a ten-minute boat ride. This time of year, we wouldn't risk it." He points one direction. "The west side of the island is lined with red mangroves. You can walk over thirty yards and still be in shallow water." Over near your hut, there's a cove where the water becomes deep quickly. It's a great place to dock larger boats during the busy season. It's also perfect for swimming and fishing."

Swimming and fishing? Jenn mouths with uncertainty in her eyes.

"What kind of fishing?" I ask.

"Lionfish are the best. Just be sure to cut off their spines."

"We'll remember that," Jenn says to Miguel. And then, leaning toward me, she whispers, "Please only fish in that well-stocked refrigerator or freezer. I'm certain in this temperature it will defrost quickly."

"Oh, isn't this vacation about adventure?"

"No, it's about our marriage. I'd like to make it home without either of us being poisoned by a fish or spider."

Miguel laughs. "Our country is beautiful. You'll be safe. Enjoy what nature has made."

We continue to follow as Miguel carries our suitcases, one on each shoulder, until the trees part to a stunning, wide white-sand beach. Our feet sink as we trod out to a wooden pier. The clip-clop of our sandals is lost in the sound of waves as we walk out on the wooden dock that leads out to a thatched hut. The pictures in the brochures and online didn't do justice to the reality. Suspended above the water on solid wood stilts, our home for the next ten days is exactly what I imagined —paradise.

With each step upon the wooden planks toward the hut, my anticipation builds. Excitement is mixed with uncertainty. This adventure will make or break our marriage, and with everything inside me, I'm hoping we come away closer than before.

Jenn's dark hair blows about her face as the breeze from over the sea whips around us.

"It's absolutely stunning," Jenn says, voicing my thoughts, as Miguel opens the door to the hut and we walk inside.

Turning a full circle, I take in the large living area complete with a kitchenette. Off to one side is an archway leading to the bedroom. In the center of the bedroom is a large canopy bed, protected by mosquito netting attached to four solid posts. The walls to the ocean are missing, replaced with only flowing white curtains bellowing in the wind.

"Is it safe to have this all open?" Jenn asks.

"Yes, ma'am," Miguel replies as he goes to the side of the opening and tugs out a wall on wheels. "You're welcome to pull these closed if you'd like more privacy or in the case of rain, but as I said, other than when we stop —and when we do, you'll hear the helicopter—you two will be the only ones on the island."

When she turns back to me, there's something in her expression that I haven't seen in too long.

"This is just what the doctor ordered," she says with a smile.

I know at that second what I'm seeing.

Hope.

I'm not only seeing it but feeling it too.

These ten days are our last chance. Our forever is

riding on it, and I plan to do everything I can to avoid a trip back to Jonas's office.

"It is," I say, leaning down and kissing her smile.

"Your refrigerator is stocked, and there is more food in the center building we passed up on the hill. There are fresh sandwiches and fruit ready for you in case you're famished after your trip. Also, in the main building on the hill, there's a wine cellar and a well-stocked bar. You may eat or drink anything you find. If you need anything..." He walks to a table near the far corner of the living room and lifts a round microphone attached by a curly cord to a large box. It reminds me of the CB radio my grandfather used to have. "...just push this button and call."

He demonstrates. "Cabin six. Cabin six calling Narvana."

"Cabin six. Narvana here." The voice coming from the box is gravelly.

"Mr. and Mrs. Masters are safely to their bungalow. They've declined a cook and know about the flag. I'm about to head back."

"Very good. Cabin six is set for ten days. Welcome, Mr. and Mrs. Masters."

Jenn and I smile at the box, knowing we could only respond if we were the ones to hold the microphone and push the button.

"Over and out," Miguel says, hanging the microphone back on the side of the radio.

"If there is nothing else, I'll leave you two alone. It's

customary for either me or one of our other tour guides to check on guests within the first twenty-four hours. So... we'll see you tomorrow?"

We both nod. "Thank you, Miguel."

I try to offer him a tip, but he refuses. "No, Mr. Masters. This is your vacation. Everything has been taken care of. Enjoy."

Jenn and I stand looking out at the stunning view until we hear the whir of the helicopter fade into the sounds of the sea.

I reach for her hand and pull her close to me. "Jenn, I want to make this work. I think we have a chance. I hope you agree."

She lifts herself to her toes in her now-bare feet and gives me a chaste kiss. "I thought I was all right with our decision. It wasn't until we were faced with those papers that I unexpectedly realized how much I don't want a divorce. I want a chance."

"Oh, baby," I say, wrapping my arms around her waist and pulling her even tighter to me, her body flush with mine. "That's what this trip is all about."

CHAPTER THREE

Jenn

I close my eyes and allow my body to simply react.

It's been too long.

It seems as if recently I've overthought everything—every action...word...everything—between Paul and me. The process is exhausting, and I'm too tired to continue. I don't know what will happen over the next ten days. All I know is that I want what's in front of me.

Forget that.

I want what's intoxicating me—my husband's embrace, the spicy scent of his skin, the way his erection probes my tummy through our clothes, and the sweet sensation of his kiss.

Sex may not save our marriage, but damn, right now as our kiss deepens, I'm on fire. Like a field of grass that's withstood a drought, the flames grow. Small explosions detonate throughout my body—tiny flares roaring to a blaze and blasting our world. Each is a reminder that there's been only one man who has ever made me feel completely and utterly loved, worshipped, and satisfied.

The one man who is with me now.

A moan escapes my lips as Paul reaches for the hem of my sundress and lifts it over my head. Just as quickly, he tugs off his own shirt, and I'm surrounded by his strong arms. His wide chest smashes against my breasts, and our hearts work together, the presence of the other increasing their rhythm. The faint taste of the salt air lingers on my lips as I kiss his neck, chest, and torso.

His body stiffens as he speaks. "Take me out. I want to watch you suck me."

I'm taken aback by not only his command but also his unfamiliar tone. It isn't like I've never given him head, but it's always been my doing. This feels different, scary, and yet somehow inviting. The strange dichotomy twists my already-tightening muscles, the ones growing painfully taut by the second. "Paul?"

His eyes darken as he shakes his head and presses a finger to my lips. "No, Jenn. No talking." His jaw clenches, the muscles in his neck bulge, and his Adam's apple bobs as he seems to weigh his next words. "We both know that this time together is it. We're walking away from this island with no secrets. We've both been keeping them. No matter what happens, it's time to let them out. Right now, my secret is that I want you to suck me...like a good wife."

A good wife?

"I-I..." I stutter my response as within a millisecond I recount our entire sexual history. It's been good. I've been happy, but never has he ever acted this way. I know exactly what he wants, what he's doing. I've read about it. I've done more than read about it. I'm not sure I'm ready for this from him. Before I can give it more thought, Paul's shoulders go back as he seems to grow larger before me.

"On your knees, baby. Now."

There is a strange duality in his command. Though it doesn't invite refusal, it's also the voice of the man I love and trust.

I fall to the floor, my panties—my only remaining clothing—dampening with desire as my nipples harden. I don't have time to process my body's reaction to his behavior before my fingers do as they were bid and unbutton his shorts and release his cock as I open my lips. Musk fills my senses as he takes over. With his fingers wrapped in my hair, he moves in and out of my mouth. Each thrust goes farther than the one before.

Though my scalp screams from the way he's holding my hair, my attention is on him and the growing need between my legs. With one hand holding his cock, I reach down to the crotch of my panties, hoping to relieve the building pressure.

Paul steps back, the loud pop filling the air as he pulls

away from my lips, and my eyes grow wide as I'm met with his stern and unexpected expression.

"No." The word hangs in the air, a heavy weight crushing me until he finally speaks again. "No, Jenn. You're only allowed to touch yourself if I tell you to. Your pleasure comes from me. Only me. Just as mine comes only from you. No more jerking off in the shower for me or your fingers finding your own clit. That's over. This is the only way our marriage is going to work. When we want something, we have to tell each other."

His heavy cock bobs with need before my eyes as he reaches for my hand and helps me stand.

I bite my lower lip as his words hit their target. It's what our counselor had said. She was right and so is he. "I'm just not used to you—"

He doesn't let me finish. "Get used to it, baby. Tell me what you want."

"I want you. I'm so..."

His lips find my neck as he once again pulls my long hair, exposing more of my vulnerable skin and my squeal fills the space between us.

"...You're so *what?*" his deep voice questions. "Tell me. Tell me what you are."

"Horny...turned on...please...I need you..."

I can't say more as his kiss lands possessively upon my mouth, and his body pushes me back onto the bed. As I bounce and crawl backward, he reaches for my panties and pulls them down my legs until the place I want him to be is exposed.

"Show me," Paul demands.

I don't hesitate as I move my knees apart, giving him a view of what he wants to see. I do it willingly, hoping that soon I too will get what I want. My eyes close and back arches as two of his fingers find my opening.

"Oh, damn, you're soaking wet."

"Please, Paul, we haven't made love..." The truth is that it's been nearly a month. What used to be good has become a bargaining chip that neither of us has chosen to barter or perhaps it was that we both found the cost too high.

I writhe under his touch as he curls his fingers inside me. My mind fills with memories of the two of us as my body warms and tingles. He works me like an instrument that only he can play, until my full body tenses and he removes his fingers. The loss is an immediate void, but before I can complain, he leans over me with his cock teasing my thighs and folds. I wiggle, trying to get him where I want him.

"Is that what you want, Jenn, to make love?"

"I...yes...Paul, stop doing this."

He sits back. "You want me to stop?"

"No, God, no. I want you to do it."

He shakes his head as he pushes my knees higher and eyes my most private area. His lips curve into a smile, yet his eyes remain dark. "Seeing your pink pussy all shiny and wet, I don't want to make love."

My chest clenches as I try to understand his meaning.

Before I can make sense of what he's saying, he leans

down and sucks my clit, sending my body into overdrive. Shouting out, I reach for the covers as heat floods my circulation and goose bumps blanket my skin. Again, his fingers find my need. "No," he says, his fingers resuming their earlier rhythm. "I don't want to make love. I want to fuck you like I've never fucked you before. I want to spend the next ten days making you hear me..." He adds another finger, causing me to gasp, before pulling them out and viciously rolling my clit between his fingers. The pleasure he's creating edges on pain as he tightens my insides like the winding of a top. "...even when I don't speak."

More taunting and my mind and body are at odds.

He leans over me until all we can see are each other's eyes. "And I want to hear you, even when you don't speak."

I'm trying to comprehend, to hear what he's saying, but my body is winning the war and my mind can't stay focused.

"Right now," Paul goes on, "without talking, your body is telling me it wants the same thing that I do."

Hell yes!

He moves over me again, his thick, hard cock poised at my entrance. "One answer, Jenn, choose it well. Do you want us to make love like two married people, or do you want me to fuck you?"

I don't even think about the consequences of my answer as I blurt out my desire. "Fuck me."

A scream echoes out to sea as in one thrust he fills me

to the hilt. There's no ease or finesse, and I've never been so turned on. My nails threaten to penetrate his skin as I grip his shoulders and take the man I've made love with hundreds of times. I take him, willingly allowing him to ravage me in a new, powerful, and dominating way. This isn't making love. It's fucking, and my body is about to explode with pleasure. My legs stiffen and toes curl as he pushes me higher, fulfilling his need while awakening ones I'd buried.

With each gyration of his hips, my orgasm builds until I'm at the precipice. It's my voice I hear begging him to never stop and my hands holding on to him for dear life, afraid that when I fall from this height, I may never find my way back.

CHAPTER FOUR

Paul

*M*y wife is absolutely stunning with her strained neck that's peppered red from the abrasion of my facial hair and her swollen lips poised into the perfect 'O' as her orgasm builds. I lift myself up on my hands and bend until I can suck one of her nipples and then the other, pulling each one taut with a quick nip that each time causes her to flinch. The quick movement sends shock waves to her core and then to my cock. It's the best example of chain reaction I've ever experienced, and I'm fascinated to see what else I can do to make it happen.

All of our love life I've worked to keep her satisfied. Of course, I came too. But that's not all that I want anymore. I want more. I need more. Having her body at my complete disposal, I am reminded of what it was like before we met, when I fed my need to dominate. I squelched that desire for Jenn, afraid it wasn't what she would want.

I'm still not confident.

Dr. Kizer told me to be honest with Jenn. I was afraid it would push her away. I told myself that I didn't need control in our lovemaking.

That lie has eaten away at me until it nearly lost me the love of my life.

Now on this island, it's all or nothing. I've opened the gate, and I couldn't stop the flood if I wanted to.

Jenn's nails pierce my shoulders, and her pleas fill the air, drowning out the surf as I continue to tease her, taking her to the brink and backing away.

Hell, my wife is a strong, intelligent woman with a career and ambitions. I don't want her barefoot and pregnant. I love her drive and determination. What I want, what I *need,* is to be her everything when it comes to satisfying her desires as she should be in satisfying mine.

I slowly ease out as her eyes open wide.

"Don't...what are you doing?" she asks, her blue eyes widening in question, their stare demanding answers even louder than her voice.

I brush a rogue strand of hair away from her beautiful face. "You're perfect. I want to keep fucking you."

Her hips move beneath me. "Then do it. I was almost there."

My grin grows at her desperation. "Baby, think about it. What do I want?"

Her chest heaves as she lets my question register. "You wanted me to suck you. You want that now?"

I laugh at the way her tone grows higher with desperation. "That's right. You suck me and once I'm done, I promise I won't leave you hanging."

She shakes her head and mutters something about not understanding, yet slowly, she moves until she's off the bed and kneeling on the floor.

I walk around her—once, twice. "Hands behind your back. I don't want you taking matters with yourself into your own hands."

With her eyes staring straight ahead and an expression of exasperation, she does as I say.

"Grab your own wrists and don't let go."

I wait until she complies.

"How's your orgasm, baby?"

"Gone." Her tone is flat.

I lift her chin until her gaze is back to mine. "Don't worry. I promise you'll get it back. Now open your lips and lower your tongue. I misled you. I don't want you to suck me. I'm going to teach you how to let me keep fucking you. Just this time, instead of your greedy pussy, it'll be your mouth."

It's as if the wheels are turning in her head. Her shoulders move backward in defiance, yet her mouth opens and tongue falls down. Though my voice is commanding, internally, I'm amused at her obvious conflict and pleased with her decision to comply. "That's it. Now take me and don't back away."

My cock, glistening with our juices, slides over her lips and tongue until I'm as deep as I can go. Instead of moving, I wait as she wiggles, fighting her own need to release her hands and take some control. Finally, her jaw relaxes, and there's a rush of air from her nose. "Baby, you've got this." Slowly at first, I rock into her, allowing her body to meet mine, our movements in sync until my balls grow tight and the need within me is too great to hold back.

Capturing the sides of her face between my palms, I thrust in and out until the tension breaks and stars explode behind my closed eyes. It's the best fucking orgasm I've had in years as I hold her in place, and she quickly swallows gulp after gulp as I continue to come.

When I'm finally done, I linger in place as she licks me clean, returning my erection. Helping her to stand, I praise her obedience while kissing her lips and tasting our tart combination. "You were perfect; now it's your turn."

"I'm not sure—"

I stop her with a finger on her lips. "I'm sure. Pleasing me is what you want. It's why we're together. It makes you hot and turns you on. I guarantee you're wet and tight and ready to snap because that's what we do. We know one another better than anyone else. Now lie back on that bed and spread your legs. I promised you an orgasm and, my gorgeous wife, I plan on delivering."

She's never been sexier than she is right now, her blue eyes wide, filled with uncertainty at my change in behavior, yet trusting because deep down she knows I'd never do anything to hurt her. She's my entire world, and it's time she takes a place in the parts of that world I've kept hidden.

"I only want to hear your sexy sounds," I say. "No words. Do you understand?"

She nods as she crawls higher onto the bed and sighs as she lies back, moving to the position I demanded.

With her beautiful dark hair fanned over the pillow and her legs spread, I begin at the inside of her knees with kisses and nips until it's difficult for her to keep from fidgeting as she bites her lip to keep from calling out. It's as I lap and lick that her sounds, moans, and whimpers grow louder.

I circle her tight ring of muscles with my thumb as my tongue continues its torment.

It's a good thing we're alone on this island because as my thumb breaches that ring, penetrating where I've never gone before, she cries out even louder. With my other arm, I hold her hips in place as she squirms and pants until her body detonates under my grasp. Once her muscles begin to relax, I prove to her what I'd said earlier: pleasing one another is the best aphrodisiac.

My dick is as hard as steel as I climb up her voluptuous body, and for the second or third time, bury myself balls deep into her warm haven.

"Paul, I don't think I can..."

"I know you can. This time, baby, let's make love?"

Her tired eyes sparkle as she looks up at me. Her gaze

is filled with more adoration and appreciation than I've seen in over a year. The expression she's giving me makes me want nothing more than to guarantee that this will all work: our marriage, our needs, and our future.

But I can't, not yet.

Jenn is the woman I chose to tone down my desires for, but how could I? How can I dial down needs when she's the only woman I desire?

I can't help but hope that I can somehow make her see that we can have both.

Her back arches as she accommodates me. "I love you, Paul. I never stopped."

"I know." I still as our eyes say things we have had trouble voicing. We're doing what I said, communicating without words. "Jenn, let me show you what I need and while I do, you tell me what you need."

Her neck strains as she reaches up to kiss me. "I need you to love me."

"I do. I love you. You're the only woman I've ever loved."

I'm sure she must be tender from before, yet she doesn't complain as we gently and slowly move together. The new wave builds until we're holding on to one another and then fall hand in hand, our fingers and bodies intertwined as we find our ecstasy together.

We remain connected, her face tucked into the crook of my neck and her heart beating below mine until our breathing evens.

She's simply spectacular, and she's mine.

I wrap my arms around her and in that moment know what I've known since the night I met her. I want everything with this woman. I want her to be strong, and at the same time I want to dominate this side of her and take care of her. She's mine in every way.

Easing us apart, I climb out of the bed.

Leaving her for only a moment, I make my way to the bathroom and dampen a washcloth with warm water. After tending to Jenn, I pull the covers over her, close the mosquito netting around the bed, and promise to return.

A short time later, I'm back with the sandwiches and fruit Miguel had mentioned as well as bottles of water. Naked within our netted cocoon, we eat and drink as the sun sets over the water, blues growing darker until the sky fills with stars.

"I can't believe we're here," Jenn says as she takes another drink of her water.

"We might come up with something fancier for dinner tomorrow."

Her grin grows. "This is the best turkey sandwich I've ever had. I didn't realize how hungry I was."

I lift a small slice of pineapple and bring it to her lips. "We must keep up our strength." Without hesitation, they part, accepting my gift.

Before she can speak, I lean in and kiss her, licking the sweet pineapple juice from her lips. "Because that's the best pineapple I've ever tasted and I plan on doing a lot more tasting through the next ten days."

Her long lashes flutter as a warm pink glow fills her cheeks.

With all of our needs met, the remnants of our food removed, and the sound of the surf our soundtrack, Jenn snuggles against my side.

Kissing the top of her head, my nose twitches from her tickling hair. There are so many things I want to say, and I will. But at the moment, there is only one that truly seems important. With my arm tucked around my wife, holding her to my side, I say, "I love you."

"You were right." Her sleepy eyes look up at me as her neck cranes on my chest.

"About loving you?"

"About secrets. I have them too." She settles her cheek against my shoulder. "But loving you isn't one of them. I do. I always have." She turns away just before her body goes limp, and her breathing creates a rhythm, telling me she's fallen asleep.

Running my hand over her soft skin, feeling the warmth of her breath on my skin, I decide to give her statement more thought in the future. We have nine more days. No need to explore everything the first day.

The glistening stars lighting the waves around our bungalow is the last thing I see as my lids grow heavy, and I join her in sleep.

CHAPTER FIVE

Jenn

*a*s I stretch on the soft sheets, my body cries out with tender reminders of what Paul and I did last night. Not ready to face the bright sun beyond my closed eyes, I keep them shut and recall my confession before falling asleep last night.

I admitted to having secrets.

That was step one. Step two is where I'm not sure I can go. I'm not sure that I'll be able to admit what those secrets are—or were. After last night, I'm not confident I know if they're past or present.

Paul's unexpected display of dominance last night did more than give me numerous earth-shaking orgasms. It rekindled fantasies I hadn't entertained since before meeting my husband. My infatuation with submission started innocently enough. Growing up, I'd never heard of anything like it. And then when I was in college, I started reading novels about role play and BDSM. While my first instinct was to roll my eyes, thinking it was ridiculous, with each chapter or new story, I found myself more and more intrigued.

My parents raised me to be strong and independent. When I read the first novel, I was on the fast track to finishing my bachelor's degree. Due to the number of advanced courses I took my senior year of high school, it would be complete in three years versus four. The plan set before me was to complete my master's degree before my twenty-third birthday.

I was the president of various organizations and clubs. I believed in equal rights, equal pay for equal work, and a woman's right to control her own body.

I still believe all of that.

Yet reading scenes of submission and domination continued to fascinate me. Thank goodness for my e-reader. I could read anything from the most well-known books on BDSM to more risqué ones, and no one would know. It was my secret.

Until.

I met him at a party my sophomore year. Richard was one year older than me, pre-med, big in his fraternity, and came from money. He was cocky and arrogant—the exact opposite of the type of man who had ever caught my eye.

And yet he did.

With his devilish green eyes and dark hair, he caught many a girl's eye. For some reason, he wanted me, and

Richard was one of those people who got what he wanted, when he wanted, how he wanted.

You know the type.

He also pushed every one of my buttons in the most annoying of ways, but most importantly, though I thought they were buried deep in my e-reader, somehow Richard saw my hidden desires.

This isn't a story with a happy ending.

He used that insight and capitalized upon it.

It started slowly. One night after too much alcohol, I agreed to being bound. The next time he added a crop. My consent became unnecessary in his mind. Before I knew it, everything escalated. My boundaries blurred until my fantasies became a recurring nightmare.

It wasn't only in the bedroom that he exercised his control. It was everywhere and everything. My appearance was under constant scrutiny—clothes, hairstyle, makeup, weight—and so was the food I ate. A simple assessment that my skirt was too tight would result in a crash diet of 700 calories a day.

My goals no longer mattered. There was only one that was important: to be a doctor's wife. For that, I didn't need the master's degree. I didn't need anything other than to be exactly what Richard said—correction, exactly what he *wanted,* even if he didn't say.

I was expected to know.

What had started as fun in the bedroom became abuse in every aspect of my life. And yet, in the center of the storm, I didn't see it. Without my fully realizing it, his degradation became my norm. Along the way I became lost.

During our relationship, I'd wake in a panic, assessing everything. I was constantly concerned that perhaps I'd unknowingly done something the day before to upset him or fearful that I would do something that day. I didn't spend as much time studying as I did worrying that one word or one look would set him off.

I knew that if it did, if I misbehaved, what at one time had been fun would become my punishment. He had the ultimate say in my—everything.

It wasn't until my parents insisted that I join them on a family vacation—showing up at our apartment and forcibly requiring me to go because Richard didn't approve—that I even realized how far I had fallen. Thank goodness my mother intervened. At first, I was too embarrassed to admit the intimate details of Richard's and my relationship—on the surface we appeared perfect. That was the only acceptable appearance. However, she and my father somehow saw through the charade.

Once I admitted the truth, my parents came out swinging. Not at me, but at him—the man I thought I'd marry.

It took time. At first, Richard was too shocked that I would dare to leave him and acted as though he didn't care. My relief was short-lived when he began following, harassing, and finally threatening me.

In the end, I transferred colleges and filed a

restraining order. I believe it was his family who convinced him to back away. Their name was well known. They didn't want little unimportant me to become a blemish on his promising career.

After all that I had gone through, I thought that I'd never trust a man again.

And then I met Paul.

The attraction was immediate. Deep down I was afraid, but it was unnecessary. Paul was nothing like Richard. Paul was fun, genuine, and loving. When we were together, life wasn't all about *him* and keeping him happy. With Paul it was about two people making each other happy and working out our differences if one of us was upset. We talked as a couple.

It's what our therapist wants us to do on this getaway.

Paul has always encouraged my career, never demeaned me or my choices. He's supported my decisions, never overruling them, and I've done the same with his. We've always been a partnership—until we weren't.

My heart starts to beat faster, recalling last night and the tone of his voice as he demanded a blowjob.

I take a deep breath and clutch the sheet wrapped around my body as I remember.

No. That wasn't what happened. Paul didn't demand. He reminded me of his desire.

Is that the same thing?

As I contemplate, I also remember how my body reacted, the way my core tightened as he pumped his cock in and out of my mouth and how wet I became. There is no denying that I was turned on.

Admitting my fantasies scares me. I did that once and it didn't turn out well.

My closed eyes work to contain tears rapidly building.

I tell myself that I don't want what Paul and I have to change, but then I recall Mr. Miller's office and the divorce papers. If things don't change, that is where we will eventually end up. Things need to change, but is this possible track the right direction?

I've never told Paul about Richard. We both know that we weren't each other's first. We agreed to keep it at that. Besides, I've always been ashamed that I'd allowed the situation with Richard to progress to where it had. After it was over, my parents insisted on my seeing a counselor. I did, for years. The counselor repeatedly emphasized that I had nothing to be ashamed of. I was the victim of a psychotic abuser.

That's what he was: not a Dom but a sadistic abuser, and though I don't have my degrees in psychology, I believe *psychotic* is accurate.

It took me a long time to fully understand that Richard had the problem, not me.

And now there's this change in Paul—his tone, his control—and the way I responded.

Damn. My body hasn't exploded with orgasms like those in years. It wasn't just one. Last night, I lost count.

I'm scared to go down the path Paul presented. While I still recall the way my body twisted and tingled at the change in his voice, I'm scared to rekindle those fantasies.

The bed shifts as my mind moves from the past and last night to present.

In a microsecond I remember fear. That same overwhelming concern I felt with Richard. Will Paul be upset? Did I do something wrong?

And then I open my eyes.

With the bright morning sun as a backdrop, I'm basking in the adoring brown-eyed gaze of my husband. Washed away by the light of day, my anxiety dissipates.

His long fingers gently move a strand of my hair away from my face, slowly passing over my cheek, as his smile broadens. "Good morning, sleepy head. Do you plan to wake today?"

Trying desperately to live in the moment and forget the past, I force a smile, blink to adjust to the brightness, yet never let my gaze leave his. "I probably should. I need to pee."

His deep laugh reverberates throughout the room as the sound of surf makes my need greater.

"Well," he says, "while you're doing that, I'll get the coffee ready. We still have fruit left from last night and I found muffins. Come out to the deck and we can decide what we want to do today."

My cheeks rise in a sincere smile.

Decide what we will do today.

Paul isn't Richard. He never will be.

"Yes," I say, wincing as I move. "I will. You'll need to fill me in on our options."

He reaches for my arm. "Baby, are you all right?"

I smirk as I answer. "I think I'm a little sore."

Paul winks. "Well then, one of our options is postponed."

It's my turn to laugh. "Postponed, not cancelled. I think I like that option, damn the consequences."

He leans in and gives me a kiss. "That's my girl."

At the sound of his praise and claim, my chest grows tight with desire. Not for sex, though I want that too, but for this—for the familiarity and understanding that our marriage provides.

CHAPTER SIX

Paul

The deck at the front of the thatched hut is covered in lattice, filtering the sun's rays as the rolling waves cause a rhythmic sway to the structure that I hadn't noticed until this morning. When I woke, I decided that after last night, I'd let Jenn sleep. While she did, I walked the entire perimeter of the island. The other huts weren't locked, yet they were as Miguel said, unoccupied.

I stopped at the main building and retrieved a few supplies to carry us through most of the day. There's still unexplored land up the hills of the interior. From the helicopter I think I saw a waterfall.

When I returned to our hut and she still wasn't awake, I made coffee.

Before waking her, I stood for a few moments

watching her through the netting. I say it often, but I think my wife is one of the most beautiful women I've ever met. I thought that from the moment I saw her across the room at a party I'd been wrangled into attending. Awestruck is a good description of how I felt that night.

Despite our recent discussion of divorce, that feeling hasn't changed. It has grown. I know that she's more than externally beautiful; my attraction is also to her inner beauty. Her heart is pure. Knowing that causes a bit of a twinge of guilt. Will exposing her to my desires tarnish her goodness? Perhaps that's why I never admitted them before.

With Jenn's long hair tousled around her face and the thin sheet covering her luscious body, it was all I could do not to strip and rejoin her in our bed. And then I noticed the subtle changes as her expression twitched.

My guilt intensified.

Was she dreaming about last night? Was it a nightmare? Was it upsetting her?

As I woke her, I saw the glistening tear, and yet her expression upon seeing me didn't warrant crying. I tried to convince myself that it was simply waking to the bright sun. Yet the possibility remains that perhaps I'd pushed too hard last night.

Our timetable is limited, and while I don't want to force her, I will show her what I need. I've done this before and understand that there's a fine line. Thankfully, I know how to navigate. We'll take this journey together, or we'll separate knowing we've been honest with one another.

I turn and smile to the soft sound of her footsteps over the wood decking.

Her gaze is out to the ocean as her blue eyes grow wide. "Paul, this is absolutely paradise."

Rising, I wrap my arms around her waist and pull her closer. "Only because you're here."

"No, I'm pretty sure this is paradise no matter what."

I tease the edge of the silk robe she's now wearing. "I think if you'd left this robe in the suitcase, it could be more of a paradise. I like the idea of my wife naked."

Her cheeks rise. "If I did that, I think that postponed item on our agenda would be moved up the schedule."

Just the thought reroutes my circulation, making my dick twitch. "Would that be so bad?"

Slowly she steps back, her lids growing heavy as her cheeks fill with color, and she reaches for the sash of her robe. "I think flexibility is the key to a successful agenda." With one tug, the sash is untied and the white satin falls open, revealing the masterpiece God created.

"Jenn, the next time we make love, it isn't going to be sweet." Her breasts heave with each of my words. "And I don't think you're ready."

Her lip disappears behind her teeth like it does when she's thinking.

I step forward and free her captive lip with my thumb, holding tightly to her chin. "Trust me?"

She nods, moving her head as much as she can in my grasp.

"Then give me this," I say. "Give me the next few days to show you what I desire, and if your needs aren't the same, we'll go back to the real world knowing we were honest."

More tears escape her eyes. This time, I don't ignore them. "Talk to me."

Her head shakes as she rapidly swallows.

Taking her hand, I lead her to the table with our coffee and fruit until she sits. "You said you trust me, right?"

"Yes."

I remove a blindfold from the pocket of my gym shorts. Stepping behind her, I begin to place it over her eyes. Immediately, her back stiffens as she sits taller and reaches up to the blindfold. "No, please, Paul. I-I..."

Not tying it, I lean down and begin kissing her neck. "Baby, trust me."

"I'm scared."

"You're intrigued." When she doesn't respond, I give her more kisses, leaning over her from behind, my lips peppering her neck, behind her ear, and down to her collarbone. Her head rolls until it falls to the side granting me access. Through the thin satin, her nipples pebble and goose bumps cover her exposed legs. "Do you want me to stop?"

"I need to know you will."

The tone of her voice and honesty of her response

cuts me, stilling me in my tracks. There is fear in her voice like I've never before heard from her.

Is she really scared?

I move in front of her and drop to my knees. "Jenn, give me your hand."

Without hesitation, she does. I place the blindfold in her grasp. "Tell me what's happening, what you're thinking."

More tears fall as she looks at the blindfold, yet she doesn't speak.

"I promise you are in control. I want to use that blindfold to show you what I mean."

Her hand clenches the black material as her gaze is glued to the fabric. I'm not sure what will happen if she can't do this simple thing. I suppose we could agree to disagree and admit that our marriage is beyond repair.

I understand fear because if this doesn't work, my greatest fear will come true. I will be devastated. Finally, she opens her hand and extends the blindfold my direction.

With a sigh of relief, I retrieve the blindfold. "Good girl." I stand and slowly cover her eyes. "Tell me what you're thinking?"

With her eyes covered and a deep sigh, she answers me with the only answer that has the power to destroy our marriage. "I'm thinking that maybe we should admit defeat."

"Is that what you want?"

She shakes her head.

"Do I scare you?"

"You? No. The way you're acting? Yes."

"What can you see?" I ask, adjusting the black material to fully cover her eyes.

"Nothing."

"What do you hear?"

She's quiet for a moment. "The ocean. I can feel it too. We're swaying."

"I recently noticed that, too."

Her lips turn upward. "I hear you."

"Good, listen to me and use all your available senses." I reach for a piece of pineapple and tease her lips. "Just trust me. Can you do that?"

Her breathing hitches. "Yes."

"Open your mouth."

She does as I say and I place the juicy fruit on her tongue. Piece by piece, I feed her. A bite of fruit and then a piece of muffin. Intermittently I add the warm rim of the coffee mug. With each step she complies. After a bit, I ease the robe from her shoulders, and she whimpers.

"Baby, you're beautiful."

"Paul, this is...uncomfortable."

"You're right. My dick is so hard, I'm hurting."

That makes her smile. "Maybe I can help you?"

I kneel again in front of her and push her knees apart, seeing her glistening pussy. "No, baby. I'm calling the shots."

Her muscles clench, but with my position between

her legs, she can't close them.

Taking another piece of pineapple in my lips, I straighten my back and drag it over her tits, leaving a trail of sweetness. Slowly, I run it downward until I tease her clit with the sweet coolness. Her moans fill my ears. Then I sit back up and bring it to her lips. "Taste it. Taste how much sweeter it is with your juice on it."

She obeys.

I begin retracing my descent, this time licking her skin until my tongue is deep inside her and she's squirming upon the chair.

I'm in control and I like it.

Control doesn't have to mean pain; it can also mean pleasure. Even when she calls out my name, I don't stop. Lick by lick and suck by suck, I push her higher. The gyration of her hips and the way she's gripping the arms of the chair, tell me what her words aren't forming.

With her vision gone, she's at my disposal for whatever I plan next.

When I lift her legs to my shoulders, she falls back. "I've got a great view of your pussy."

"Paul, please..."

I swirl her clit with my tongue, drinking her juices. It's as I use my teeth that her legs begin to stiffen.

"Paul, I'm...I'm..."

"Do it," I command.

Jenn screams as her body trembles and quakes. With her still panting, I stand, wrap the robe back around her and tie the sash. By the time I remove the blindfold, we're both smiling.

I wink as I sit across the table from her. "Would you like some more coffee?"

She shakes her head. "Coffee? After what you just did, you're asking me about coffee?"

"Yes, my love, coffee."

Her eyes search me, hopefully seeing me in a way she's never seen me before.

"Coffee?" I ask again, lifting our empty mugs.

"Yes, I'd get it," she says, "but I'm not sure my legs work."

"If their job is being a vise, they work. Baby, you were squeezing my head." I stand and get the pot of coffee from the coffee machine. When I return, I kiss the top of her head. "Don't worry. You'll have plenty of opportunity to service me."

Though I see a bit of concern, overwhelmingly, her expression is one of satisfaction and satiation.

As I sit, I ask, "Would you like to call for an excursion or stay on the island?"

"What else is there to do on the island?"

"If I say all there is to do is fuck, will you choose the excursion?"

With the cup to her lips, her eyes find me. "Most definitely not."

"So my wife is okay with riding my dick all day?"

She shrugs. "I mean, we also need to eat."

CHAPTER SEVEN

Jenn

*I*t turns out that there is more to do on the island than make love. With our hands joined, we continue our walk exploring the beach. The walk isn't only to enjoy the beauty of the island but to do what Dr. Kizer recommended, to talk.

"Paul?" I ask with my toes in the sand and the sea breeze and sun on my face.

"Yes?"

"Do I need a safe word?"

He stops in his tracks with our hands still joined.

Looking back from where we've come, I notice our footprints in the sand and wonder about this change in my husband. Can we go back, and do I want that?

"How do you know about safe words?"

"Books," I answer honestly. Richard didn't believe in

them. He said a true submissive would never use one anyway. He said he could choke her until she was at death's door, and she wouldn't ask her Dom to stop. It was his way of conditioning me, telling me exactly how to behave.

I was probably at that door more than once.

I push those thoughts away as I concentrate on my husband's silly grin.

His smile grows as his eyebrows raise. "So you've read about submission?"

I nod. "Not lately, but I have. It's in a lot of romance books."

"What are your thoughts?"

"I told you. I'm scared."

He sits on the sand with his long legs bent and his bare feet near the shore's edge before he tugs my hand for me to join him. "Then what you read is wrong."

"Wrong? What do you mean?"

"I told you there have been secrets in our marriage. Here's mine. Before you, submission was what I looked for in a woman. I was attracted to women who were submissive at heart." He squeezes my hand.

My pulse increases, remembering how Richard said he knew that about me before I did. "Before me?"

Paul's smile gleams from his shining dark eyes to his bright white teeth. "Jenn, I know you're a strong woman. I love that about you. This isn't about every aspect of our life. I thought I could give up my need for dominance to be with you. It's worked in every part of our relationship except our sex life. I miss it. I want it. I want you to at least try it."

I'm trying to listen to him with an open mind.

Damn Richard for doing what he did. What should be fun is tainted.

My opinion is skewed and I know it. I've read books where what Paul is describing works, where participation is a mutual decision. Because of my past, I worry that those instances are only fiction. "Why did you say what I read was wrong?"

"Because if you trust me, there's nothing to be frightened about. Remember breakfast?"

My cheeks rise. "I do."

"How about last night?"

"I remember last night."

"Good," he says with a laugh. "What happened to you while you were pleasing me, letting me fuck your mouth?"

I look down at the print on the sundress I'm wearing over my bathing suit, suddenly fascinated with the swirls of color. Because if I look at my husband's face, I know I'll be embarrassed to admit the truth.

"Jenn?"

"I was turned on. Like more than I can remember being."

"And after?"

My head shakes. "I don't even know how many times I came." I look up. "What about a safe word?"

"Will you use it?"

I take a deep breath. Is he asking if I'm a true submissive? "I don't know. If I did, would you stop?"

"Are we talking about the act or everything? Are you asking if there's a word that will mean that you tried this and you can't do it—any of it—and you want out of our marriage?"

"I suppose that word is *divorce*, but I want to know if there's a word to stop what you're doing, not one to end *everything*. A word that will simply give me voice to be honest. I don't want to be physically or emotionally hurt."

Paul nods as he looks out over the ocean. "Damn, Jenn. You have given this some thought."

"I told you, I've read books. Sometimes it ends well. Other times it doesn't."

"Can you define hurt?"

"I don't know. Some of the things I've...read about seem intriguing."

He takes a deep breath as his bare chest rises and falls. "When I first got involved in BDSM, I had a mentor. He—"

"A man?" I ask, surprised.

"Yes, a man. We didn't have sex. He was a regular at a club I frequented. I could talk to him. He told me something that I'll never forget. He asked me the difference between hurt and harm."

I can't believe we're having this conversation after six years of marriage, and yet I'm not only anxious, I'm impressed. What Paul is proposing is more than a whim.

He actually understands it. "You learned how to do this?"

He shrugs. "I believe I was born with the desires. I learned how to do it right." He turns his gaze to me. "Can you answer the question my mentor asked me?"

"The difference between hurt and harm?" I ask, confirming his question.

"Yes."

I give it some thought. "For me, I think hurt means pain."

"What does harm mean?"

"Intentional...irreparable."

"Intentional? If I spanked your sexy ass, there would be pain. It would be intentional. Would it be harm?"

My nipples harden and core twists as I imagine what he's asking. Damn my body. No matter what my mind thinks, its traitorous responses give me away.

His gaze falls from my eyes to my breasts. I can tell by his grin that he sees the way they've reacted. "Maybe we should give it a try?"

"No."

Paul's brow shortens as his eyes widen in a look of surprise or shock. "No?"

"No," I clarify. "It wouldn't be harm. It would be hurt. That's physical, which is most usually reparable. I also said emotionally and that's different."

He nods. "It is. What scares you about the emotional side?"

"Losing me."

Paul sits straighter and reaches for my cheeks, pulling me closer. With our noses nearly touching, all I can see is the brown of his eyes. "Baby, that's what this is all about. I don't want to lose you."

Before I can respond, his lips are on mine and our kiss grows deeper. He tastes of coffee and saltwater. There's more I want to ask, more I want to say. I know if this is going to work, I need to confess my secrets too. I wonder if our initial attraction was because of my secret and his. Apparently, it was there, though neither of us confessed.

Many questions flit through my mind. None of them lasts long enough to find a voice. I'm too overwhelmed with the man taking my breath away, the man making me forget everything else, the man who doesn't want to lose me.

"I told you," he says between kisses, "that the next time we fucked it wouldn't be sweet."

He begins lifting my sundress, his fingers on the side of my bikini bottom. "I meant it, but right now, I want to make love to my wife. We can fuck later."

With the way my insides are twisting, I know it's what I want too. It's also what I need. It isn't only the desire, though that's strong. It's the connection. "Yes."

I barely have the word out when Paul is inside me. My back arches as I whimper and try to adjust.

"Baby, you're so wet and tight."

Thrust after thrust, on the white sand and in the bright sun Paul fills me. Our bodies, familiar with one another, join in the way that's meant to be. Like two pieces of a puzzle made for one another, we fit perfectly together. This is the man I fell in love with, the one who makes sweet love to me.

I fist the sand as we move in sync and the pressure builds. Sweet and attentive, he takes me higher. Up we go above the clouds. I'm on the edge when in the distance a rumbling roar grows louder.

Paul stops, still inside me, and our gazes meet. "Helicopter," he says with a chuckle.

"Miguel said they fly over multiple times a day."

Paul's grin grows. "So my wife doesn't mind being fucked in front of others?"

I do mind. I know I do. That's not how I answer. "We aren't *fucking*. We're making love."

As the roar grows louder...

"In that case." He resumes his movements. In and out. I'm not sure if it's the sun or our activity, but as the roar begins to fade, the heat within me intensifies. It's as the sound is almost gone that Paul's neck strains and we both come.

My orgasm isn't the explosion of last night. Instead, it is something deeper, a reassurance that things can change and yet remain the same.

With perspiration covering our skin, Paul rises from the waist, and our eyes meet. "Helicopter," he says with a grin.

"I'm glad it flew over."

"No. Helicopter is your word that means stop for now."

I nod.

"Divorce."

Even hearing him say it makes my stomach twist. "I don't want to say that." *Please don't push me to say that.* I don't say the last part.

"I don't want you to, but that's your decision, not mine."

"You will really give me that control?" I ask, chuckling that we're still connected and yet carrying on this conversation.

"Baby, you have the ultimate control. Like I said, your books misled you. And next time, before we fuck?"

"Yes?"

"I'm going to spank your round ass."

I want to say *helicopter.* I want to, but by the way Paul is smiling, I know he can feel the way his promise—or threat—caused my core to clench. Since it would be a lie to deny that the idea does something to excite me, I simply reply, "Yes, Sir."

His lips crash with mine as our tongues dance.

I'm not one hundred percent sure of this choice, but I can't argue with the way I react. I have to tell myself that this is different than before. I love and trust my husband. Maybe our attraction has always seen the other sides of one another. It's just our consciousness that finds it unexpected.

CHAPTER EIGHT

Paul

"*Y*es, Sir."

My dick rebounds, growing hard at those words coming from my wife. It is either that or the way her pussy is gripping me. While we were talking, her orgasm faded and she relaxed. And then when I promised to turn her sexy ass fire-engine red, her entire body shot to alert.

The part of me that didn't think Jenn would go along with this is quickly disappearing. She is uncertain and rightfully cautious, yet she isn't offering any resistance.

I pull out, knowing she's got to be sore from last night and now. "Turn over, baby. On your hands and knees."

Without hesitation she obeys, leaving her sundress around her neck and her sexy ass in the air. Reaching forward, I tease her clit and pussy until she's writhing and moving to my touch. I keep taunting as my fingers slide in and out, curling to provide the perfect friction and then back to her swollen bundle of nerves.

I love the way she reacts, so honest and pure. I could watch her come all day long, but that isn't my goal. As her breaths shallow, it's her way of letting me know she's on the edge. I change my rhythm as she wiggles and shakes.

"Please," she begs.

I lean over her back, my hard dick close to its desired destination as I move her long hair away from her face. Peering into her glassy eyes, I gather her locks and move them to her other shoulder, giving me access to that sensitive skin behind her ears. With my breath on her flesh, in my domineering tone, I whisper, "How did I never realize how greedy you were?" Before she can answer, I say, "We just made love. What are you asking me for now?"

"You," she says, her word more of a pant as her bikini-clad breasts sway.

"It's not that simple. I told you there was a price to pay before we fucked. Do you remember?"

Her head bobs and eyes close.

"You can't have my cock again until I make that ass red."

"I-I know."

"And you want that?"

Her beautiful eyes blink before zeroing in on me. "I trust you."

"Baby, when I make that sexy ass red, it's going to hurt."

"I-I know," she says as tears fill her eyes.

She's fighting with herself. I can hear it in her voice. She's scared, but thank God, she's also turned on. It's the perfect combination. "Do you still want me to fuck you?"

"Hmm," she says, more of a purr.

"Stand up and take off the rest of your clothes."

As she obeys, my gaze devours every inch of her body, slowly scanning from her toes in the sand to her long, flowing hair and every curve in between. From our excursion today, her skin is pink, kissed by the sun. But up until now, her breasts were covered. As she removes her bikini top, my suspicions are confirmed. Not only is she wet, but her tits are heavy, also showing her wanton need with the way her nipples are hard and a deeper shade of red from the rush of blood.

I walk closer. "I love your tits."

"Thank you, Sir."

That word is better than any blue pill. Taking a step back, I grip my length and run my grasp up and down. "I'm all slippery from your wet pussy."

Jenn nods as she looks at my cock and then away.

There are so many things I want to do to her. I want her on her knees, my fingers wrapped in her hair as I control her air and she surrenders to my whims. I want to fuck her in the ass, the one place I've never gone. I want to feel the vise of her muscles on my dick. I want to take her back to the hut and bind her hands before I spank her ass.

Each image in my imagination adds to the blood supply in my dick.

Walking around her, I take in the curve of her ass and imagine my handprint on that bright white flesh or a bright red welt from my belt.

My hand moves faster. I'm so hard, my balls ache.

Walking back to stand in front of her, I run my free hand over her cheek as I continue stroking my length. "I'm so fucking hard right now. If I told you all the things I want to do to you, you would run away. You should run away."

Her nipples grow harder, puckering with the pressure. "I-I don't know what you want me to say."

"That's your choice. Say whatever word comes to mind because if you don't, I'm going to make you wish you had."

"Paul."

She whimpers as I tweak one of her nipples, pinching and twisting. Yet she doesn't pull away.

"Are you afraid of me?"

"You won't hurt me."

"Oh, baby, I want to."

Her blue eyes meet mine. "I know. I guess what I meant to say is that you won't harm me."

"Never. I'll take it slow," I say as I lead her to the

trunk of a tall palm tree and direct her hands in front of her. "The bark is sharp, so don't bend your elbows.

"I don't have my belt to redden your perfect ass."

She makes a small gasp as her head falls forward at my confession, and I notice how her nipples harden. She may be nervous, but her body is defying her.

"This time," I go on, "I'm going to use my hand. Move your legs farther apart and show me that sexy round ass."

Jenn's toes wiggle as she spreads her legs, preparing for my punishment. As I run my hand over her skin, warming it to lessen the sting, her muscles flex beneath my touch. We're under the shade of the tree, but behind me are the beach, ocean, and sun. As Jenn spreads her legs, the sunshine highlights the glistening cum on her upper thighs. Damn, she was wet before, but it's more evidence that I'm not the only one turned on.

Letting her know that I see her desire, I spread her essence between her ass cheeks. "You're so wet. My wife is naughtier than I knew." She doesn't respond as I move higher, letting my finger circle where I've never been. She sucks in a deep breath. "What's your safe word?"

"Helicopter." Her toes continue to flex.

"Your other?"

Jenn shakes her head. "I don't ever want to say it."

I take a step back. "Hold on, baby. You're going to feel this."

Her fingers blanch as she tightens her grip on the tree.

I can hardly believe we're this far, this fast. It has been my dream, my fantasy.

And now it's reality.

I rear back and with my open hand slap her ass as she cries out.

Fuck yes!

My hand tingles in the most invigorating of ways. Beneath my gaze, her skin rises and reddens in the shape of my hand. Without warning, I do it again on the other side. Her head falls forward with the second spank, yet she doesn't lessen her grip.

I run my palm over both cheeks. The inflamed flesh turns my dick from hard to steel. This little taste of what I can do has me wanting more. I imagine her entire ass red as flames. However, currently I have a more pressing matter. If my dick gets any harder, it may break off.

Reaching for her hips, I thrust inside her ready core in one mighty action.

"Oh!" she calls out.

I grip her hipbones tighter as I thrust again and again. In and out. The friction builds as my balls pull toward me. Purposely, I lean into her. With each gyration, my pelvis slaps against her recently spanked skin as a reminder of what I've just done. By the sounds she's making, the reminder is working.

My fingers ache with the grip I have on her, yet I can't let go. It's fucking heaven pounding deeper than I've ever been. The mounting need within me builds, not only in my groin but all over. Perspiration coats my skin. If I were a pressure cooker, I would be about to blow.

Everything has disappeared except Jenn and me. Her moans and pleas push me faster until our bodies are slamming against one another.

We're alone in a tunnel—the island, the ocean—and all that is around us are gone.

Instead of moving away from the pain she must feel on her ass, she's moving with me. Since this began, her cries have changed, now turning to gasps as she climbs her own mountain.

I'm reminded of what I'm doing. For these ten days to work, I need to help her, train her. One of the lessons she needs to learn is that when we're in these roles, my pleasure is the focus, unless I choose otherwise. Denying her an orgasm is within my power.

At the moment, my pleasure is at an all-time record high, and there's only one reason. It's because I'm not fucking a nameless submissive from a club. This is better than any sub I've ever had. This is my wife. Having her come also brings me pleasure.

Just as I'm about to explode, I release one of her hips and reaching forward, find her clit.

Like a strike to a match, she detonates as her pussy clamps down. It's the final straw and my world ignites. With my arms now wrapped around her, keeping us both upright, stars flash—make that fireworks—behind my now-closed eyes. I let out the roar I've kept suppressed as my dick convulses, filling her to overflowing.

"Oh God, I-I can't..." she stutters as her body loses its rigidity.

I wrap my arms tighter around her waist, showing her that she's safe in my embrace.

When I pull out, I turn her in my arms until she's facing me. Lifting her chin, I take my thumb and trace the trails of her tears. "Baby, you know your word."

"I do," she says, swallowing more tears. "Thank you for letting me come. I was afraid you wouldn't."

My lips curl upward. "I was wrong. Your books haven't completely misled you."

CHAPTER NINE

Jenn

It wasn't books that misled me. I don't say that.

It's difficult to say much of anything as I float back to reality from that earth-shattering orgasm. I had forgotten the intensity that pain adds to pleasure. With just two slaps to my ass, I remembered why I liked this kind of play before it was ruined for me.

Unsure I can remain standing, I lean into my husband's chest. The beat of his heart sounds in my ear as he hugs me tighter, surrounding me with his familiar fragrance and reassuring embrace.

Stroking my hair, he says the words I need to hear. "I love you, Mrs. Masters. I'm so proud of you. I can't believe that you're..." His words trail away.

Taking a deep breath, I respond, "I love you, too." Looking up, I take in his expression. Without his words of praise, I would know how he felt with his eyes. The adoration is glowing from his face. "May I ask you more questions?"

Paul laughs. "I want you to ask. I want you to understand."

"You've done this before? Domination?"

"Usually with more than a few slaps with my hand to an ass."

How has he been like this and I didn't know? "But not since me? Why?"

"No, not since you. I would never cheat on you. I guess...it's hard to explain, but you didn't seem like..." He shakes his head. "When I met you, I was head over heels in love in a way I'd never experienced."

My cheeks rise.

"You were everything I had never thought I wanted. Successful, strong, and independent. Yet I was drawn to you. You seemed so pure—"

"Paul, you know I wasn't."

He puts his finger over my lips. "That's not what I mean. I don't care that you had been with someone else. I had too. I meant, pure as in genuine. I was afraid if I showed you my desires, I'd darken you in the process."

"You're not afraid of that anymore?"

"There's only one thing I'm afraid of."

I tilt my head. "What?"

"Losing you. And it almost happened." His grip of my waist tightens, reminding me of how he held me as he fucked me. I won't be surprised to see bruises in the shape of his fingers. "We were there, at Miller's office. The papers were in front of us. I was too close to losing you."

Tears fill my eyes again, not from physical pain, but audible. I hear the anguish in his voice. "I thought that was what you wanted. It was a mutual filing. You weren't...we weren't...happy."

"No. It wasn't happiness that was the problem. It was honesty. That's what Dr. Kizer said, and she was right. She said we needed to be honest about everything. The first time she said that, I knew that this was what I'd held back. I admit, I thought if I told you, you'd run. And then things progressed. We had pens in hand, and I knew that if we didn't face my secret, our marriage was over. The thing was...in Miller's office, it was over. I figured we had nothing more to lose and everything to gain. I had to risk darkening your purity."

"You could never do that."

"I didn't tell you before because I didn't want to scare you away."

I contemplate what he's saying, including the advice from our counselor about honesty. "It would have," I say honestly. "Six years ago, it would have scared me but not for the reason you think." Six years ago, I was still recovering from my experience. Six years ago, I would have run, like Paul told me to do earlier. I try to explain. "This scares me now, but we have history, and I know you." I shrug. "Well, I thought I did."

His brown eyes glow as he loosens his grip and

reaches for my left hand, lifting it higher until he kisses my knuckles. "You do know me. I'm the same man you married."

I smile as he wiggles my wedding band. "Assuming we avoid my end-all word, how is this..." I motion toward the tree. "...these desires of yours... how will it affect our relationship at home?"

"What do you mean?"

"You said you liked me the way I was. You were attracted."

He kisses the top of my head. "I love you, your drive and ambition. I'm stinking proud of all you've accomplished at the firm. I wouldn't be surprised if you made partner. You're amazing at everything you do.

"I even enjoy your stubbornness. Baby, our marriage is a partnership. I don't want a Stepford wife. I don't even need this every time." He tilts his head toward the beach. "I love my wife, and I enjoy making love to her. I also like punishing her ass and fucking her. I want the woman I married in every respect, with ultimate control in the bedroom."

Heat fills my cheeks as I relive what he just said. With a deep breath, I ask the million-dollar question. "Is it possible to have it all, to have it both ways?"

He shrugs. "I guess that's up to us."

"To *us*," I repeat. "You're saying that this can be our private, behind-closed-doors playtime, but everyday life will be the way it's been? You won't start telling me what to wear or how to do my hair?"

He chuckles lightheartedly, reminding me that he is the man I married.

"Nope, baby, you don't want fashion advice from me. And I like the way your hair is right now."

I run my hands over my head, pushing down my hair. "It's a mess and there's probably sand in it."

"But I know how it got that way, so I like it. And as for clothes, the only fashion advice I'll give is for you to take them off."

I shrug. "Well, tan lines are a pain."

"Speaking of pain, how's your sexy ass?"

"It's sore."

"Your pussy?"

My smile broadens. "Incredibly satisfied." And so is my heart.

Is it possible to have both? I don't know. However, I do know that for the first time in a long time, I have something else. I have hope.

As Paul bends down to pick up our discarded clothes, my sundress and our swimsuits, I consider volunteering to dress as he suggested, or rather, not dress. However, before I can, the roar of the helicopter returns, making us both peer upward from the trees. This time, it doesn't seem to be flying over. The whirring roar grows louder and louder.

Though we're hidden from the pilot's view by the trees, soon we won't be.

"Maybe I should take your fashion advice another time," I say.

Paul smiles and hands me my bathing suit. "I plan on keeping your naked body to myself, so my advice is that we both get dressed. It seems as though we have a visitor."

I never understood the desire to share me. I hated it, yet by the time it happened, I was too far gone to dare to protest. The strange thing is that I don't recall the other men, what they looked like or what they did. I only recall how degrading it was for Richard to watch and critique.

I close my eyes.

"Give it to her in the ass. She likes that, don't you, my pet?"

My stomach twists, recalling his words and tone, bringing back images I'd tried to forget.

With another man's cock inside me, he'd lift my chin. "I didn't hear you." He'd speak to the man. "Keep going." And back to me, "Pet, you were asked a question."

Despite what was happening, I learned to hear only him. "Yes, Master."

"Jenn," Paul calls my name, his voice coming from what seems like a distance until he reaches my shoulders and pulls me closer. "Honey, are you all right? You're suddenly pale."

I shake away the memories. "I-I…"

He pulls me tighter, and I still in the security of his embrace as the roar grows louder. I lift my chin until our gaze meets again. "I'm well, Sir." I grin hoping that he will be all right with that title. And then I giggle.

"What's funny?"

"Our last name."

"Our last name is funny?"

I tilt my head. "Masters?"

"I guess that plural 's' means we both are because, baby, like I said, you're in control."

My voice rises as the helicopter hovers over the beach. "And I'm glad you don't want to share."

"Never."

Once we're dressed and the helicopter is nearly landed, I reach for Paul's hand. "My ass is sore, but I trust you. The only time I plan on saying the name of that flying machine over there is when it's really here."

"Flying machine?" he asks with a chuckle.

I shrug. "I don't want you to get the wrong idea."

As we walk toward the helicopter, Miguel removes his earphones and waves.

I lean toward my husband. "Do you think he saw us earlier on the beach?"

"It may be why he didn't land then. But if he did, I'd guess we aren't the first couple."

I take in the beautiful scenery. "Or the last."

CHAPTER TEN

Jenn

*O*ur days and nights are filled with one another. From hiking to the interior of the island and swimming in the fresh water of a waterfall to lying on the beach, we enjoy paradise. Throughout it all, we play with Paul's fantasies. One by one, he reminds me how much better this kind of relationship can be with someone you trust completely.

It's finally after six-plus days on the island that I summon the courage to open up to my husband, not sexually—I've never been more open. I want to open up emotionally and share my past. I don't know why I'm frightened, but I am. With all his talk about honesty, I'm afraid that he won't understand why I didn't tell him any of it before. During the entire day, I think about our pending conversation, how to break it to him that what he considers his dark secret isn't new to me.

I settle on after dinner.

In the late afternoon everything changes.

The wind grows stronger as the previously consistent crystal-clear sky turns dark. From the security of our hut's deck, I watch as churning multidimensional clouds roll, swirl, and billow, filling the horizon with uncharacteristic gloom.

For a moment, I wonder if it's a sign, telling me not to confess.

With my thoughts lost in the brewing storm, Paul's embrace from behind catches me unaware. His strong arms wrap around my waist, and his broad chest stabilizes me, giving me an anchor against the gusting winds.

"It looks like we're in for one of those storms they warned us about. One of the reasons that this time of year is off-season."

I shake my head, not wanting the storm or the uncertainty that the clouds bring. "Maybe it will pass." I crane my neck, turning to look up at my husband. "Besides, Miguel hasn't flown over yet today."

"Oh, I don't think he can in this weather. We're good on food."

I shrug. "I know. I guess I like predictability. It makes me uneasy when things aren't how I expect."

Paul reaches for my chin, turning my body toward his as the wind whips my long hair around our faces. "Are you talking about the weather or us?"

"The weather," I answer honestly. "And Miguel's visit." My cheeks rise. "I guess I like him to land; that way I know that once he's gone, we're guaranteed privacy."

My husband's gaze goes out to the churning sea and clouds. "I would suspect that we can guarantee privacy."

"Cabin six, Narvana here," the alien crackling voice calls from the two-way radio.

My eyes widen as I peer into the hut and back up at Paul.

"Cabin six, Narvana here."

Other than the first day when Miguel showed us the hut for the first time, the two-way radio has been silent. Until now.

We both rush toward the radio as the same message comes through, this time with more static, the words garbled.

I reach for the microphone. "Cabin six," I say.

"Cab...storm...secure hut...main building."

My eyes widen as I look to Paul.

He reaches for the microphone and speaks louder. "Cabin six. Narvana, you're breaking up."

"Wind gusts ... over sixty miles per hour. Go...main building."

"Right away," Paul says as a strong wind gust blows things from the center table.

A flower arrangement crashes, the vase breaking as water and flowers litter the floor. Paul runs for the walls and begins to tug them closed as I work to clean the mess. Once the glass is swept, I turn my attention to my husband. He's closed and secured a few of the sides, but not all. There are more. Working together we make our way around the perimeter to enclose the structure. With the way the walls are shaking, it's clear that the man on the radio was right.

We need to get to a more permanent structure.

It is then that a large wave crashes against the hut. We both stumble as the hut sways and water rushes from under the movable walls, seeping inward and spreading over the interior floor boards.

Paul quickly pulls our suitcases from the closet. Together, we gather our belongings, the ones we don't want to lose—my purse, our iPads, and our passports. Without thinking, we throw miscellaneous odds and ends in our suitcases. At the last second, I decide to include pillows and a blanket. I've been in the main structure, but I haven't looked around enough to know if there are cots or anything for spending an undetermined amount of time.

As I reach for another blanket, Paul taps my shoulder and speaks over the roar of the growing storm. "That's all we can carry. Leave the rest. We need to get to the main building."

I nod. Looking around as a crack of thunder rattles the hut and lightning flashes through the openings in the thatch, I begin to wonder if the hut will survive.

Will we?

Did we save our marriage only to lose our lives?

"You're right," I say, closing my suitcase and securing my purse strap around my neck.

With his computer bag and suitcase in tow, Paul opens the door that leads to the pier. More water rushes in as wind rips the door from his hand. The door blows inward, crashing against the wall. "Come on," he screams, his voice disappearing into the storm.

We struggle to make it to land, the dock that before was a perfect row of rounded planks is now covered by a torrent of water threatening to wash us into the sea. The relief of the beach is short-lived. Each step through the sand is like walking in quicksand with the added danger of flying debris. Palm fronds, sticks, and leaves swirl around us.

A walk that normally takes us five minutes extends to nearly twenty as we trudge, eyes down, protecting ourselves from the pelting rain and dangerous debris. As the wind speed increases, simple objects are turned into missiles. Partway up the hill, we stop to catch our breath and survey our surroundings.

"Leave your suitcase," Paul says. "I'll leave mine too. The only thing that matters is getting you in that building."

I shake my head. "No. What if we lose everything?"

Though we're screaming, our voices are barely heard over the roar of the storm.

"I'll come back and get them once you're secure."

I reach for his hand. "I'm not losing you for a suitcase. Either we get them there or we don't. But we're not separating."

In the midst of the storm, Paul smiles. "Never."

"Never."

"Give me yours," he suggests. "We're almost there. You concentrate on walking. I'll get the suitcases or I won't. We need to keep going."

I nod, passing him my suitcase.

The muscles in his arms flex as he grips the handles.

He was right. The sheer size of both of them makes them more like sails than a place to store belongings. If we were on a cement path, we may be able to use the wheels, but that's not the type of path we're on. The once-packed ground is now a river flowing from the top of the hill down toward the beach. Not only are we fighting the wind, we're practically swimming upstream.

When we finally make it to the main structure, Paul pushes the door inward until it's wide enough so we can enter. As he releases the handle, the door flies inward as leaves and sand litter the floor. Once we're both inside with our suitcases, he uses his shoulder and body weight to push the door closed.

We both stand, soaked and trying to catch our breath as the storm seems to lessen.

It's an illusion.

Through the windows it's evident that it is still raging.

However, within the building made of concrete blocks, it's as if we hit a mute button.

The only amplified sound is the beat of the rain as it pings against the metal roof. Our saturated clothes and soaking wet hair drips onto the concrete floor, creating puddles and adding to the mess that blew inside with our arrival.

I look over at the door. "Can you lock it?"

"I don't think so. But we're the only people here and the wind can't open a door that's latched." He turns to me, placing his hands on my shoulders. "Are you all right?"

I nod. "Wet, but fine."

He shakes his head. "That came up so fast."

"I'm glad we're here. I'm afraid the hut won't make it."

"I don't care about the hut. I only care about you."

My body shivers as the chill from the wetness seeps to my bones, and I lean against the warmth of his body. We remain still, listening to what we can no longer feel until he says, "Let's look around. I never really checked this place out except to get food or a bottle of wine." He tilts his head to a rectangle on the floor. "That's the wine cellar. I think this place is stable, but if we are worried, we can always go down there." When I nod, he goes on, "Let's see what else there is."

Taking my hand, I follow my husband as we move from room to room.

The building isn't large, but then again, it's bigger than the hut. The rain continues its beat upon the roof as we step into the kitchen, complete with numerous refrigeration and freezer units that we know from experience are filled with food. There's also a large stove and multiple ovens.

"The brochure says something about a chef," Paul says. "I would guess had we wanted one, this is where he would cook."

"Or she," I say with a smile.

"Or she," Paul agrees.

I let out a sigh of relief when we open a supply closet. It's filled with large white fluffy towels, washcloths, soap, and even hair care samples. "I may have to wash my hair in the rain, but now at least I know I can."

There are also blankets, sheets, and pillows, as well as a washer and dryer. "I forget this island could have three huts full of people," Paul says.

"I like it the way it is."

He winks, his hair still dripping. "Me too."

There's another supply closet with tools and equipment used to maintain the buildings and tropical landscape. "I'm sure they're much busier in the heart of the tourist season."

The last door we open is similar to a studio apartment, and the sight of the living quarters makes me smile. "I wonder if this is where the chef stays?"

Paul drops my hand and walks farther inside. Along with a small kitchenette, there is a sitting area, bedroom, and an attached bathroom. It's not nearly as luxurious as the bathroom in our hut, but it has a shower and at this moment, that sounds like heaven.

I shiver again at another crash of thunder. "I'm cold. Do you think we can take a shower during a storm?"

"It depends on the pipes."

When I narrow my eyes, he continues, "If the pipes are PVC—plastic—they can't conduct the lightning."

"If they're metal," I volunteer, "they can."

"Right. And we don't know." Paul goes back to the supply closet and grabs two towels. "I'd rather that we play it safe for now and dry off. I didn't lose you in the storm. I don't intend to lose you in a shower." Before I can say anything else, he adds with a grin, "And after you take off those wet clothes, I'll come up with some other way to warm you up."

I'm not sure how he's able to make my insides flutter and nipples tighten with only words and a smirk, but he does.

CHAPTER ELEVEN

Paul

*L*eading her to the bed, I help her remove the wet sundress and then each piece of sexy bikini beneath. With the towel in hand, I dry her body from her sexy legs to the top of her head and everywhere in between. It's as we cuddle under the blankets with her soft, warm curves against me that my erection grows.

In the middle of the storm, I do what I said was always my option. I make love to my wife, soft and gentle, until we both climb our mountains, our bodies twisting tighter and higher than the storm clouds.

Perhaps it was the hike against the wind and rain, the adrenaline from the storm, or the orgasm, but whatever the cause, after we are both satisfied, Jenn's eyes close and she drifts to sleep.

Now, a few hours later, after eating some fruit and

cheese, my mind goes to my other option. Gentle was right for our arrival. Now we're settled and safe, and my thoughts are on a different kind of play.

Before we left the hut, I made sure to bring a few things I'd brought along from home, some surprises she'd yet to see. I'm determined to take this slow but steady. Jenn's already come so far—and so many times.

Okay, that's two different meanings of the word, but I thought I'd throw it in there to emphasize that I'm not pushing her on this. I'm leading and she's following with equal enthusiasm.

The storm continues to rage beyond the walls, and while the rain on the roof is loud, after a while it fades to background noise. I suppose that's how it is when people live near a railroad track or an airport. The mind gets used to the sound, and slowly it forgets to register.

It's as the windows rattle with the occasional gust of wind or the thunder cracks and lightning flashes that Jenn shivers again.

"Baby, we're safe."

"I know," she says, but her tone doesn't match her words.

"I have an idea to keep your mind off the storm."

Her lips curl upward. "I think I know what you're thinking."

"See, we're doing what Dr. Kizer said."

"Having tons of sex? I missed that in her therapy sessions."

"Oh, it was there. You just weren't listening. Now you are."

She looks up from the chair where she's wrapped in a blanket with a Kindle in her hand. It's where she's been since she woke earlier from her nap. "You're right. I'm listening and so are you."

"Trust me?"

"Implicitly."

"Then come here," I say, standing from the couch where I've been sitting and walking into the bedroom where I've already set up my surprise.

Wrapping the blanket around her, she follows. When she gets to the doorway, her steps freeze as she sucks in a breath. The fear that washes over her expression nearly breaks me. I'm not trying to frighten her but heighten what we have.

"No, Paul."

I reach for her hand. "You know your word. Do you want to say it?"

She looks up at the solid chain I found in one of the supply closets. While she was reading, I lassoed it over an exposed beam. If it hadn't been for the rain, she would have heard the clatter. I then secured a pair of soft, wool-lined wrist cuffs from the end. It's at the perfect height where she will still be able to stand with her legs spread, but her arms will be forced upward. Her lip disappears behind her teeth as her eyes grow moist. "What are you going to do?"

"That's where the trust comes in."

She spins my way. "I don't want to say my word."

"Then trust me," I say as I tug at the blanket she's wearing. When she doesn't respond, I tilt my head toward the bed. "If you're not ready for the ceiling, I have some bindings for the bed.

Jenn nods with an audible sigh. "Yes...okay...May we start with the bed?"

"Drop the blanket." The change in my tone is her warning.

Without hesitation she obeys, the blanket pooling at her feet, leaving her sensual body completely exposed. She lowers her chin and drops to her knees.

She's so fucking sexy. My dick comes to life.

But I want her bound.

Giving her my hand, I say, "Good girl, come on. We'll start with the bed."

On shaky legs she stands and obediently follows me to the bed, awaiting my instruction.

"Lie down on your back and lift your hands over your head."

With a deep sigh, she does as I ask, adjusting until her arms are stretched over her head. In that position, her tits are on full display, reminding me of a pair of nipple clamps I have tucked away in my suitcase.

As I secure the satin rope around her wrists and tug against the metal headboard, thunder crashes making Jenn jump.

"We're safe," I say. She hears my words, but her beautiful blue eyes don't believe it. "Repeat what I just said."

"We're safe."

I reach for the blindfold we've used a couple of times since the first breakfast. Instead of being frightened, Jenn's cheeks rise.

"Your word?" I ask as I bring it toward her eyes.

"No."

I tweak one of her nipples, painfully pinching it as she squirms. "That isn't an acceptable answer."

The blindfold is now in place.

"I'm sorry, Sir. I don't want to say my word."

"You know not to use the word you just did, don't you?"

"Yes, Sir."

"When I'm in control, *no* isn't an option. Your safe word is, but never no."

"I'm sorry, Sir."

"Roll over. I think you need a reminder."

The bed moves as she squeezes her thighs and attempts to roll. The simple movement is complicated by the bindings as well as the loss of sight. Instead of helping, I enjoy watching her struggle to comply. Eventually, she is where I want her, on her elbows and knees with her hands extended and still bound.

"Do you know how beautiful you look?" I ask.

"N-I mean, if you say so, Sir."

She is. Her long, dark hair has streaks of light brought out by the tropical sun. It's mussed from drying in the bed after our lovemaking. The disarray gives her a wild, untamed look as if she's a vixen ready for my next command.

Running one hand over her ass, I reach for my belt buckle with the other. With the crack of my belt on her skin and in her ears, she'll forget about the lightning and thunder. Before I spank her ass, I let my fingers find her folds. The small bedroom fills with her moans as I tease. "Damn, girl, you're wet and ready. After your punishment, should I let you come?"

"Please, Sir."

"Please, Sir, what?"

Her hips writhe against my hand, trying to get friction to her clit, the place I'm purposely avoiding. She's been so responsive lately that it barely takes a tweak and she's convulsing from the inside out.

"Please, Sir, let me come."

"What needs to happen first? I need to know you're willing."

"My punishment, Sir. I'm sorry I said *no*."

Who knew my wife would catch on this quickly? Who knew she could be a submissive?

Her entire body tenses as my belt cuts through the humid air just before her gasp fills the bedroom, and the leather of my belt slaps against the white of her ass. With only one strike, her face is buried in the pillow, and a sheen of perspiration covers her sun-kissed skin.

"Think about what's happening. Nothing else."

Her head bobs.

"Listen to my voice," I say as I rear back and deliver another stripe from my belt.

The way her skin welts, immediately responding to each lash, has my dick growing by the second. After another couple of strikes, I crawl onto the bed behind her and run my palm over the raised skin. "So fucking gorgeous." And then I reach down to her core, finding her wet and ready. "You've been so good, I'll let you choose." The sound of my zipper lowering fills the air as I free my hard cock. "I'm going to fuck you right now. I don't care if I come in your pussy, ass..." I pull apart her ass cheeks and peer at the place I've never been. "...or down your throat, but, baby, I'm going to come." I run my hand over her sore red ass to remind her of what just happened. "I'm not untying you, so no matter what, you'll feel what I did to your ass."

If it's her mouth, I'll make her roll back over. She'll feel the rough blanket against her skin. If it's either other option, I'll make sure she feels me against her skin.

Jenn turns her face away from the pillow, her cheeks covered in tears as her tits heave against the bed and she catches her breath. "Please, Sir, my pussy, so I can come."

With a grin, I slap her ass again, eliciting another shriek.

"Selfish girl." Before she can respond, I line up the tip of my cock and drive deep into her tight core. There's no need to prep her: she's wetter than she's ever been.

"Oh!"

It doesn't take long with this position. Damn, the

friction from her tight cunt makes my balls tighten and stars appear behind my lids. I could withhold her orgasm, but this distraction from the storm is for both of us. I want her to reach her height too. Leaning forward and cupping her mound, I pinch her clit. That's all it takes. The stars explode as her pussy contracts, squeezing my dick, and she screams out my name.

Though it's still raging, I've lost track of the storm. The thunder and pelting rain change in intensity, growing louder and then softer. However, it means nothing. My world is wrapped entirely around the woman beneath me.

Once I'm totally spent, I collapse on top of her and her neck cranes. Tugging her blindfold upward, I reveal the most stunning blue eyes.

"Paul, I love you. I need to tell you something."

It's as I start to move that a sharp pain pricks my ass, like a bite.

Fuck!

I expect a spider or snake; instead, when I turn, there's a strange man behind me with something in his hand. I can't process what's happened. Jenn's scream is the last sound I hear before the world goes black.

CHAPTER TWELVE

Jenn

*P*aul's body falls onto mine, suddenly heavy.
Before I can process, a man with a dirty shirt
and an American accent speaks. "Well, lookie what we
have here."

The blindfold is still on my forehead, obstructing my
full view of the room. "No!" I scream as someone I can't
fully see drags Paul from the bed and throws him to the
ground.

"I thought you said there wouldn't be no one else on
this island?" the person dragging Paul says.

The dirty-shirt man responds, "I guess it's the sea
gods. They gave us a present."

The other man laughs. "And it ain't even my
birthday."

"Mine neither." Dirty-shirt man smiles a sinister, yellow-toothed grin toward me. "But, fuck, she's all tied up like with a ribbon. Sure looks like a present."

My heart is thundering in my chest, and I've pulled away, but there isn't far that I can go with the way my hands are bound. I bring my knees up as far as I can in the fetal position.

The farther man's footsteps upon the concrete floor echo as he comes closer. "My kind of gift. I think she likes it rough."

I close my eyes and vigorously shake my head as their laughter vibrates off the walls, the sound punctuated by the continued torrent of rain. Silently, I call out to my husband, wondering what they did to him and where he is. Through it all, I can't drown out their voices.

"And I thought we were going to die out there on the sea in that storm. Instead, we crashed on Fantasy fucking Island, and we get to spend our night fucking this dirty slut."

My body quakes with fear as I squeeze my eyes tighter, wishing for Paul to wake, wishing for the blindfold to be fully covering my eyes so that I wouldn't see either of these men, and wishing to be back in Wisconsin. When I open my eyes again, my stomach rolls as dirty-shirt man has his unimpressive cock in his hand.

"The first time, I'll take her ass." He looks back at the other one with that nasty grin. "You can have her mouth."

My head is shaking, silently pleading. As he gets closer, my trembling becomes almost convulsive. I wish my reaction was due to fear of the unknown. It isn't. I know exactly what they're going to do to me. I've been here before with Richard and his friends.

Then I didn't fight.

Now I want to.

As dirty-shirt gets closer, I use the only defense I have, my feet and legs, as I kick out, making contact with his thigh.

"Ow, you fucking little cunt."

And then it's too late; he's behind me, his skinny cock going straight for my ass. His lack of size doesn't reduce the pain as he shoves inside with no preparation. I fall forward, burying my face in the pillow as his slimy hands hold my hips and he ruts like the disgusting pig that he is.

This isn't like anything I was experiencing with Paul.

This is brutal and mortifying. The hot breath on my back and neck reek of whiskey and cigarettes. It's all I can do to hold back the bile threatening to move up my throat. Before I can process more, pain shoots through my scalp as my head is lifted by my hair.

The second man—I still can't see his face—pulls me toward the edge of the bed, forcing his cock toward my mouth.

"You bite me, bitch, and we kill him."

Kill him?

The only part of that sentence that means anything to me is that Paul isn't dead.

I didn't think it would be possible to endure what is happening and have hope, but as the second man yanks my head, allowing me to see Paul lying in a heap, I do.

My husband is still alive.

We will survive this unexpected detour.

I believe that with all my heart.

Time passes. It may be minutes or hours. I don't know. They've done something with Paul. He's out of the room. They also found the liquor. The only positive to that scenario is that the more they drink, the less they can get it up.

They're inventive fucks, coming up with other ways to enjoy their gift.

My pleas are few. I know these kinds of men. They get off on fear.

Somehow, as the night progresses, I find my way back to a place I once knew, where I would retreat from the world and its cruel, painful reality. Years ago, when I went there, I had one job: listen to and obey Richard. With a room full of men and my eyes covered, I zeroed in on Richard's voice.

Tonight, it's not a voice that I'm listening to. This time with the men's voices blocked, I concentrate on the rhythm of the rain on the metal roof. In the steady beat, I hear Paul's voice. The deep tenor isn't degrading like Richard's had been. It's encouraging and supporting.

"I love you, Jenn. I always have and I always will."

I believe that. I hold on to the hope that this will end and we will survive.

"I'm sorry I darkened your light."

"No, Paul. You are my light."

It's as I lose consciousness that I'm faced with the reality—we may not survive.

CHAPTER THIRTEEN

Paul

*P*ain and disorientation greet me as I slowly regain consciousness. Through closed eyes, I try to remember what happened.

Did I drink too much?

That's what it feels like—a hangover with a heavy head, throbbing temples, and a dry mouth.

I slowly open my eyes to the darkness surrounding me as memories return.

Slowly at first, it's a stream of consciousness.

There was a storm.

My body aches with a deep chill.

In the black of night, I listen. From the sound alone, it seems as though the storm has finally subsided. It's as I reach for Jenn that something within my chest clenches.

She isn't with me. I'm also not in the bed but on the hard, cold concrete floor.

Where am I?

My eyes can't adjust to the utter black of the dark. Slowly I move my sore muscles and use my hands to see, patting the concrete around me. It's as if my legs are bound. They aren't. It's my shorts around my ankles. Pulling them back into place, I realize my belt is still missing, and my chest floods with dread as my touch reaches something. A shelf.

I remember the main building.

What happened?

I'm not in the bedroom but within a supply closet.

Oh my God. Where is Jenn? What happened?

The last thing I remember she was bound to the bed and there was pain...a spider. No. A man...

Fuck!

My stomach tightens as the fear from my chest fills my entire body, accelerating my heart and prickling my skin.

My wife.

I have to save my wife.

Please, don't let it be too late.

I have no idea how long I've been out. There's no way I can even allow myself to imagine what they've done to her. If my mind slips that way, I won't be able to go on.

As I concentrate on saving her, my mind floods with questions.

Should I turn on the light? If I do, I could risk

alerting whomever put me in this closet that I'm now awake. No. I can't give him any advantage.

Instead, I continue my blind search of the closet. It's not the one with the towels or blankets. It's where I found the chains and I'd seen tools.

Doing my best to stay quiet, I continue searching until I find what I recall seeing, a long screwdriver and a sickle.

With both in tow, I reach for the door handle, certain I'll find it locked. With a prayer, I turn the knob and slowly rotate.

The door opens easily toward me, and I take a step back. The lighting is dim, but compared to the closet, it may as well be a spotlight. Squinting, I survey what I can see from my limited angle.

The room beyond is empty and eerily silent. With my heart pounding in my ears, my attention goes to the light seeping from beneath the bedroom.

One step.

Another.

I stop and listen.

Snoring? Do I hear snoring?

Pushing the door inward, I can see there's a man naked on the bed, passed out with a nearly empty bottle of whiskey in his hand.

Where is Jenn?

And then I see her.

I practically have to cover my mouth to stop from screaming.

She's no longer bound to the bed but by the cuffs that I'd arranged over the ceiling beam.

My heart aches, knowing I'm responsible for those chains.

Holding my breath, I watch her chest, the tits I love, as I silently promise God, or any greater being, anything and everything for my wife to be alive. Then it happens. The breath she takes is small, but the slight movement tells me what I need to know. She's alive, unconscious and hanging from her wrists with her face down, but alive. With an unreal sense of relief, I begin to scan her more thoroughly. Her hair is messy and covering part of her face. Behind the matted dark tresses, there is bruising. The mask that had been over her eyes loosely hangs around her neck. And then my circulation runs cold as my gaze continues downward seeing the dried blood on her legs.

I can't allow myself to consider what that man did to my wife. If I do, I could end up killing him or giving him the opportunity to kill us. I have to keep my wits.

One more step and my feet stall as a second man comes into view.

There were two?

The second one is passed out on the floor, wearing nothing but boxers.

Guilt and rage wage an internal war as I contemplate decapitating both these men. I'm not a violent man, but desperate times—desperate measures. There's no doubt in my mind that with the sickle in my hand, it could be easily accomplished. The door moves a little more and Jenn's eyes snap open.

In the split second it takes for her to find me, there are myriad emotions—fear, relief, and then shame.

When her lips part, I shake my head and bring a finger to my lips.

She immediately obeys, her eyes turning glossy as a rush of tears streams down her discolored cheeks.

It's then I recall the rope that is also in the supply closet. As much as I want to kill these bastards, having my wife watch me murder two men is more trauma than she needs after whatever they've put her through.

I lift my finger in the air, the universal sign for one minute. Though her eyes open wide, I quietly rush back to the closet and find the rope.

When I return, neither man has moved.

Silently, I tiptoe into the room, knowing if I release her, the chains may wake the men.

"Baby," I whisper and give her a kiss. "Shh. Are there more?"

She shakes her head and speaks through bruised and cracked lips. "No. Just these two."

"Okay, I'm going to tie them up first." I scan both lifeless forms. "Which one passed out first?"

She tilts her head. "Him, dirty-shirt."

"What?"

"The one on the bed."

At least with his being naked, I don't have to worry about a concealed weapon. The man Jenn referred to as *dirty-shirt* murmurs when I reach for his hands, but he doesn't wake. His stench invades my nose and I hold back a gag as I secure his wrists, bringing back my sailing days in college to tie the perfect set of knots. With another loop around the headboard, he's not going anywhere.

The whole procedure took less time and more rope than I planned, but at least I know he's no longer a threat.

I tilt my head back to the door, letting Jenn know I'm getting more rope for man number two.

Though I hear what she's saying with her eyes, that she's telling me to hurry, to be careful, and mostly that she loves me, she simply nods.

This time I turn on the light in the closet. There isn't more rope, but there are zip ties and duct tape. I can easily work with what I have. Not only did I sail, when I was younger I also made it all the way to Webelos in the Scouts. They taught us to improvise.

"Paul!" My wife's shout increases my pulse, causing me to jump as I turn toward and rush back to the bedroom.

The man who had been on the floor is standing and wobbling on the balls of his feet. His head is tilted and his eyes unfocused.

He's disoriented. Thankfully, I'm not.

Without hesitation, I dash forward, head-butting his stomach, the full force of my weight throwing him backward against the concrete block wall. His *oompf* as my move causes him to exhale and Jenn's scream fill the room. When he falls to the floor, I rear back and punch his face. My fist pummels his cheek and nose over and over.

My hand aches and he's not fighting, yet the punches continue.

This is for whatever you did to my wife.

This is for what your drunk friend did.

"Paul, stop!" I can barely hear her.

This is for ruining our perfect vacation.

This is for hurting her and scaring her.

This is for knocking me out.

Finally, above the sound of crunching cartilage, Jenn's screams, combined with yelling from the man on the bed, register. The one on the floor is unmoving and unconscious.

His face is bloody, his nose off-kilter, and there's blood oozing from his partially open mouth. The way the blood is dribbling, his heart is still pumping.

"I think I knocked out one of his teeth," I say as shock settles in.

"Motherfucker," the man, dirty-shirt, yells.

Ignoring him, I go to my wife and gently undo the cuffs as her arms fall around my neck and shoulders.

"Baby, I'm so sorry," I say, over and over.

Her body trembles in my grasp as she buries her face against my chest and her grip of my shoulders gains strength. "They...they..."

I lift her face, fully seeing her swollen cheek, darkening eye, and dry, cracked lips. "It's my fault. I didn't know anyone was on the island." I gently brush my lips against hers, wanting to tell her she's still the most beautiful woman I know, and that I'll spend the rest of my life making this up to her. However, the yelling from the man on the bed is growing louder.

"Untie me, you motherfucker."

Jenn slips from my grasp and reaches for a lamp. Without a word and stark naked, she marches toward the man.

"Dumb cunt, I should've—"

The lamp smashes down on his head, breaking into shards as his body goes limp.

"You shut the fuck up!" she screams.

I rush to her side, taking what's left of the lamp from her grasp. When she turns to me, her blue eyes are wide, wild, and filled with emotion.

"I'm not a fucking cunt," she yells, turning back toward the unconscious body. "And I'm not a goddamned pet or anything I don't want to be!"

"Jenn," I say cautiously, laying a hand on her arm, more than a little worried that my wife has lost her senses. "I'm here. They can't hurt you anymore. Are you all right?"

Her naked frame straightens and chin lifts with more determination than I thought possible. "I'm not, but I will be."

Fuck, my wife is amazing. How could I have ever ques-

tioned her ability to handle my desires? She's the strongest person I know.

I nod, pulling her close to my side as I lead her away from the bedroom. "I want to tie up the guy on the floor. Once I'm done, let's get you something to wear and leave here. The storm has stopped. We'll fly the red flag. Hopefully the hut is still there, and more importantly, the radio. We'll call Narvana and get you medical attention."

She exhales and looks down at herself. "I feel so filthy. I want a shower or a bath, but I know that's not what I'm supposed to do."

"What else do you want?"

Her big blue eyes stare up at me. "To tell you that I'm sorry."

"Fuck no. *I'm* sorry." I point back toward the room containing the two unconscious men. "My job is to keep you safe and I failed."

Her small hand reaches up to my cheek. "Do you remember my saying I wanted to tell you something?"

I shake my head, trying to clear the fog of whatever drug they gave me. As the memory returns, I shrug. "Maybe, before everything went black."

"I was so afraid they killed you."

"Jenn, can you ever forgive me? Is this it? Can we recover from this?"

When her hand drops from my cheek, she reaches for my hand. "I'm exhausted and tired and sore. If you promise you don't blame me for what happened to—"

"No!"

Her cheeks rise at my quick response.

It's my turn to gently rub her face, tracing a purple bruise as I swallow. "They hurt you."

"Without too much detail, and I know this will sound crazy, but I've been hurt worse."

My back stiffens and jaw clenches at her declaration. "Who? When?"

She squeezes the hand intertwined with her own. "Tie him up so we can call for help? Because if he still wants me, I want to go home with my husband."

"I want you. You're amazing and mine. And sometime, when you're ready, you have to tell me everything."

She nods. "I will. Do you remember how you were afraid I'd run?"

"Yes."

"So am I."

"Never, baby. Never. I love you. You're stuck with me."

"I love you, too."

CHAPTER FOURTEEN

Jenn

Thankfully, the hut was still there—damaged, but present. More importantly, the radio survived. With the storm passed, the helicopter arrived in record time, along with a boat filled with law enforcement officers. The two men who Paul tied and locked in the apartment were on an international watch list of drug smugglers and pirates.

I know what you're thinking. I thought the same thing.

I didn't know pirates still existed, not in the *'over the sea'* way, but according to the authorities, they do.

The two men who shipwrecked on our island have been busy over the last few years, robbing yachts and vacationers all around the Caribbean. While they were presumed guilty of many crimes, my charge was their first count of aggravated rape.

When the officers asked me if I wanted to press charges, briefly, I recalled Richard's justification for past situations. How I got what I deserved. How it was his right. How if I'd only learn to behave.

I could have let that stop me. I didn't. What those men did was wrong and with the help of years of past counseling and the constant support of my husband, I'd come too far not to understand the difference.

What I endured on the island may have been similar to times with Richard and his friends, but I knew without a doubt, this time was completely without my consent. And nothing is allowed to happen to me without my consent.

There was no way I wouldn't press charges. And besides, my husband was one hundred percent behind me. His support and the overwhelming evidence gave me the courage and strength to tell the law enforcement officers everything I could remember.

Thankfully, with immediate medical attention, after the police questioning, Paul and I were able to travel back to Wisconsin the very next day.

A few days later at Dr. Kizer's office-

"Jenn, you asked to be here when you talked to Paul about something you want to tell him?" Dr. Kizer asks as more of a confirmation to our appointment than a question.

I grasp my husband's hand. "Yes, I'm scared."

"First, Paul and Jenn, before the unimaginable and unexpected, how was your time on the island?"

I turn to my husband's brown-eyed gaze, waiting for him to answer. When he does, I hear the defeat in his tone. "Doc, it was going great, but now..." He doesn't try to finish the sentence.

"Can you tell me why and how it was great?"

Paul takes a deep breath. "I was honest. I told Jenn about the desires I had—*have*," he corrects. "She was doing great. Each day was building on the last." He sighs and turns to me. "I was so fucking proud of you."

Before I can respond, Dr. Kizer does. "You *were*, Paul?"

"No. I am."

"This is why I wanted to talk here," I say to Dr. Kizer. "I hope you can help me make him understand that what we were doing and what those men did are not the same."

Dropping my hand, Paul stands and paces toward the window. "I know they're not. But I was the one that tied you. Because of me you were defenseless. I hung that chain—"

"Paul," Dr. Kizer asks, "let's concentrate for a moment on the positive. Tell us, how did you feel reawakening those dominant feelings?"

"Good, but now it feels wrong."

"Not if I want it," I admit.

"But how could you?"

I take a deep breath. "You were wrong about me. Or right. I'm not sure. Maybe part of our initial attraction was our complementing desires. I'd done more than read about submission. In college I began playing with BDSM."

His eyes grow wide. "You never said anything. You were so...*not* submissive."

I take a moment and bite my lip before going on. "I was in a relationship where it got out of hand. It wasn't domination. It was abuse. He controlled everything in and out of the bedroom—my clothes, hair, and even goals. He even controlled who I had sex with." My stomach rolls as I say the words aloud.

"What? Who?" His stare locks to mine as his forehead furrows. "Is that why you asked so many questions?"

I nod.

Paul's gaze darkens. "He hurt you? Really *harmed* you?"

I nod again. "I went through years of counseling. I didn't hate submission. As a matter of fact, I like it." I shrug. "Maybe you could tell?"

For the first time since the island, my husband smiles as he comes toward me and kneels at my feet. "I thought you did, but then..." He bows his head to my knees.

"Paul." I lift his chin. "Those years of therapy helped me understand the difference. You understand this so much more than he did. It was a power trip for him. You're patient and loving. I trust you.

"Nothing you did or so far want to do is without my consent. Nothing crosses that line. And if it would, you've given *me* the power to stop it."

I look into his eyes as they swirl with so many emotions. When he doesn't speak, I continue. "The realization that we have the same correlating desires is another reason I don't want to lose you. I love and trust you. You saved me and not just on the island. You saved me from the first night we met. You showed me that when there's love, trust, and respect, submission is okay.

"You demonstrated that by more than blindfolds and spankings...by supporting me with the police and doctors, letting me tell them what happened. You also showed that you can be there for me, stand beside me when I need to be independent because I needed that closure." My voice cracks. "You told me we can have *both* if we want it." I shrug and grin through my slow cascade of tears. "Even though learning about your desires was unexpected, I am more than okay with them. I want what we can be together. I want to stay married and move into the future with you."

Instead of answering, he sits upward on his knees until our lips meet. The connection is electric and everything I need: sweetness, love, and devotion, yet also control. His hands come to my cheeks, choreographing our movement with the precision of a true Dom and I love it.

Since the island, he's treated me with kid gloves. The force as our kiss grows causes my thighs to clench as my nipples bead. Maybe I was wrong to do this in Dr. Kizer's office. If we were home, I could be naked.

When he pulls back, his eyes again contain the love and adoration I saw earlier on the island. His unspoken praise fills me with warmth.

"Paul," Dr. Kizer asks, "can you hear and accept what Jenn is telling you?"

"I do hear her." His hand caresses my cheek where the bruise is fading, as his lips curl upward into a smile. "I think she's saying she never wants to ride in a helicopter."

I giggle. "I only want that with you, and you're right, I don't. I just need to know that it's an option."

"Always."

EPILOGUE

Jenn

A *year later-*

The hut sways gently with the waves as the warm tropical breeze blows my sundress and hair. My gaze is stuck on the man standing at the rail of the deck. As I take him in, I know that not only is my husband the handsomest man I know, he's the one I love unconditionally and trust with my life. He's my partner and my Dom. He's the man who encourages me to be independent yet also gives me the confidence to be submissive.

My sight is on him. Beyond the rail, the sun shimmers on the ocean, framing his broad shoulders and tanned skin in explosions of light.

"I can't believe you were willing to come back here." Paul says, turning back toward me with a grin.

"Why not? This is where we saved our marriage. Besides, they offered us a free week with no other guests and a chef and security on the island."

Paul comes closer and cups my cheek. His nose scrunches as he speaks. "I kind of hate that."

"You do?"

"Yeah, with all those people—a chef and security—we won't be able to make love on the beach or spank your ass by a palm tree."

My cheeks warm—as well as other parts of my body. "No, but we have this entire hut for that."

His eyebrows quirk upward as desire radiates from his darkening gaze. "What did you just say?"

"We have the entire—"

His cadence slows. "Did you tell me *no*?"

A giggle escapes my lips as I think back. "Yes, Sir, I believe I did."

"Do you know what happens when you say that..." He motions around. "...in the bedroom?"

I could argue that the entire hut is kind of a bedroom, but I don't. I can't with the way the warmth is pooling between my legs. My chest heaves in anticipation of what my husband has planned as I fall to my knees. Instead of looking down, I peer upward with a ridiculously large smile across my face. "I'm not sure what will happen, Sir. That is up to you, but I'm ready."

"How ready?"

"Very ready for whatever you want."

His shoulders square as his tone deepens in the way

that sets me on edge—a very good edge. "If I checked, would you be wet."

"Soaked, and my nipples are hard."

Paul offers me his hand. "Baby, that's not unexpected."

"It's not."

After I stand, his fingers go the straps of my sundress, pushing them one shoulder at a time until the dress flutters to the floor, creating a pastel puddle at my bare feet.

Taking a step back, Paul scans from my toes to the top of my head. His menacing smile grows as he shakes his head. "Tsk-tsk. Mrs. Masters, you seem to have forgotten to wear your panties. Whatever am I going to do with you?"

I'm glad we both can keep some things unexpected.

Did you know that Paul and Jenn were referred to Dr. Kizer by the characters in UNCONVENTIONAL? If you enjoyed UNEXPECTED, please download UNCONVENTIONAL today and learn Dr. Kizer's secret of success... explore those desires!

Also, if you'd like to get a sneak peek at Aleatha's brand new dark romance trilogy, WEB OF SIN, with an alpha anti-hero who will melt your heart and your panties, turn the page and enjoy the prologue to SECRETS.

WEB OF SIN-BOOK 1-SECRETS

Prologue

Araneae

My mother's fingers blanched as she gripped the steering wheel tighter with each turn. The traffic on the interstate seemed to barely move yet we continued to swerve in, out, and around other cars. From my angle I couldn't read the speedometer, though I knew we were bordering on reckless driving. I jumped, holding my breath as we pulled in front of the monstrous semi, the blare of a truck's horn filling our ears. Tons of metal and sixteen wheels screeched as brakes locked behind us, yet my mother's erratic driving continued.

"Listen very carefully," she said, her words muffled by the quagmire of whatever she was about to say, their weight pulling them down as she fluttered her gaze between the road ahead and the rearview mirror.

"Mom, you're scaring me."

I reached for the handle of the car door and held on as if the seat belt couldn't keep me safe while she continued to weave from lane to lane.

"Your father," she began, "made mistakes, deadly mistakes."

My head shook side to side. "No, Dad was a good man. Why would you say that?"

My father, the man I called Dad for as long as I could remember, was the epitome of everything good: honest and hardworking, a faithful husband, and an omnipresent father.

He *was*.

He died less than a week ago.

"Listen, child. Don't interrupt me." She reached into her purse with one hand while the other gripped tighter to the wheel. Removing an envelope from the depths of the bag, she handed it my direction. "Take this. Inside are your plane tickets. God knows if I could afford to send you away farther than Colorado, I would."

My fingers began to tremble as I looked down at the envelope in my grasp. "You're sending me away?" The words were barely audible as my throat tightened and heaviness weighed down upon my chest. "Mom—"

Her chin lifted in the way it did when her mind was set. I had a million visions of the times I'd seen her stand up for what she believed. At only five foot three, she was a pit bull in a toy poodle body. That didn't mean her bark was worse than her bite. No, my mother always followed through. In all things she was a great example of survival and fortitude.

"When I say your father," she went on, "I don't mean my husband—may the Lord rest his soul. Byron was a good man who gave his...everything...for you, for *us*. He and I have always been honest with you. We wanted you to know that we loved you as our own. God knows that I wanted to give birth. I tried to get pregnant for years. When you were presented to us, we knew you were a gift from heaven." Her bloodshot eyes—those red from crying through the past week since the death of my dad—briefly turned my direction and then back to the highway. "Renee, never doubt that you're our angel. However, the reality is somewhere darker. The devil has been searching for you. And my greatest fear has always been that he'd find you."

The devil?

My skin peppered with goose bumps as I imagined the biblical creature: male-like with red skin, pointed teeth, and a pitchfork. Surely that wasn't what she meant?

Her next words brought me back to reality.

"I used to wake in a cold sweat, fearing the day had arrived. It's no longer a nightmare. You've been found."

"Found? I don't understand."

"Your biological father made a deal against the devil. He thought if he did what was right, he could... well, he could *survive*. The woman who gave birth to you was my best friend—a long time ago. We hadn't been in contact for years. She hoped that would secure your safety and keep you hidden. That deal...it didn't work the way he hoped. Saving themselves was a long shot. Their hope was to save you. That's how you became our child."

It was more information than I'd ever been told. I have always known I was adopted but nothing more. There was a promise of *one day*. I used to hope for that time to come. With the lead weight in the pit of my stomach, I knew that now that *one day* had arrived, and I wasn't ready. I wanted more time.

The only woman I knew as my mother shook her head just before wiping a tear from her cheek. "I prayed you'd be older before we had this talk, that you would be able to comprehend the gravity of this information. But as I said, things have changed."

The writing on the envelope blurred as tears filled my sixteen-year-old eyes. The man I knew as my dad was gone and now the woman who had raised me was sending me away. "Where are you sending me?"

"Colorado. There's a boarding school in the mountains, St. Mary of the Forest. It's private and elite. They'll protect you."

I couldn't comprehend. "For how long? What about you? What about my friends? When will I be able to come home?"

"You'll stay until you're eighteen and graduated. And then it will be up to you. There's no coming back here...ever. This city isn't home, not anymore. I'm leaving Chicago, too, as soon as I get you out." Her neck stiffened as she swallowed her tears. "We both have to be brave. I thought at first Byron's accident was just that—an accident. But then this morning...I knew. Our time is up. They'll kill me if they find me, just like they did Byron. And Renee..." She looked my way, her grey eyes swirling with emotion. While I'd expect sadness, it was fear that dominated. "...my fate would be easy compared to yours."

She cleared her throat, pretending that tears weren't cascading down her pale cheeks.

"Honey, these people are dangerous. They don't mess around, and they don't play fair. We don't know how, but they found you, and your dad paid the price. I will believe forever that he died to protect you. That's why we have this small window of time. I want you to know that if necessary, I'll do the same. The thing is, my death won't stop them. And no matter what, I won't hand you over."

"Hand me over?"

We swerved again, barreling down an exit until Mom slammed on her brakes leaving us in bumper-to-bumper traffic. Her gaze again went to the rearview mirror.

"Are we being followed?" I asked.

Instead of answering, she continued her instructions. "In that envelope is information for your new identity, a trust fund, and where you'll be living. Your dad and I had this backup plan waiting. We hoped we'd never have to use it, but he insisted on being prepared." Her gaze went upward. "Thank you, Byron. You're still watching over us from heaven."

Slowly, I peeled back the envelope's flap and pulled out two Colorado driver's licenses. They both contained my picture—that was the only recognizable part. The name, address, and even birth dates were different. "Kennedy Hawkins," I said, the fictitious name thick on my tongue.

"Why are there two?"

"Look at the dates. Use the one that makes you eighteen years old for this flight. It's the only way they'll let you fly unaccompanied. Once you're in Colorado, destroy the one with the added two years. The school needs your real age for your grade in school."

I stared down at one and then the other. The name was the same. I repeated it again, "Kennedy Hawkins."

"Learn it. Live it. Become Kennedy."

A never-before-thought-of question came to my mind. "Did I have a different name before I came to you?"

My mother's eyes widened as her pallid complexion changed from white to gray. "It's better if you don't know."

I sat taller in the seat, mimicking the strength she'd shown me all of my life. "You're sending me away. You're saying we may never see one another again. This is my only chance. I think I deserve to be told everything."

"Not everything." She blinked rapidly. "About your

name, your dad and I decided to alter your birth name, not change it completely. You were very young, and we hoped having a derivation of what you'd heard would help make the transition easier. Of course, we gave you our last name."

"My real name isn't Renee? What is it?"

"Araneae."

The syllables played on repeat in my head bringing back memories I couldn't catch. "I've heard that before, but not as a name."

She nodded. "I always thought it was ironic how you loved insects. Your name means spider. Your birth mother thought it gave you strength, a hard outer shell, and the ability to spin silk, beautiful and strong."

"Araneae," I repeated aloud.

Her stern stare turned my way. "Forget that name. Forget Araneae and Renee. We were wrong to allow you any connection. Embrace Kennedy."

My heart beat rapidly in my chest as I examined all of the paperwork. My parents, the ones I knew, were thorough in their plan B. I had a birth certificate, a Social Security card, a passport matching the more accurate age, and the driver's license that I'd seen earlier, all with my most recent school picture. According to the documentation, my parents' names were Phillip and Debbie Hawkins. The perfect boring family. Boring or exciting, family was something I would never have again.

"And what happened to Phillip and Debbie?" I asked as if any of this made sense.

"They died in an automobile accident. Their life insurance funded your trust fund. You are an only child."

The car crept forward in the line of traffic near the departure terminal of O'Hare Airport. A million questions swirled through my head and yet I struggled to voice even one. I reached out to my mother's arm. "I don't want to leave you."

"I'll always be with you, always."

"How will we talk?"

She lifted her fist to her chest. "In here. Listen to your heart."

Pulling to the curb and placing the car in park, she leaned my direction and wrapped me in her arms. The familiar scent of lotions and perfumes comforted me as much as her hug. "Know you're loved. Never forget that, Kennedy."

I swallowed back the tears brought on by her calling me by the unfamiliar name.

She reached for her wrist and unclasped the bracelet she always wore. "I want you to have this."

I shook my head. "Mom, I never remember seeing you without it."

"It's very important. I've protected it as I have you. Now, I'm giving it to you." She forced a smile. "Maybe it will remind you of me."

"Mom, I'd never forget you." I looked down to the gold bracelet in the palm of my hand as my mom picked it up, the small charms dangling as she secured it around my wrist.

"Now, it's time for you to go."

"I don't know what to do."

"You do. Go to the counter for the airlines. Hand them your ticket and the correct identification. Stay strong."

"What about those people?" I asked. "Who are they? Will you be safe?"

"I'll worry about me once I'm sure that you're safe."

"I don't even know who they are."

Her gaze moved from me to the world beyond the windshield. For what seemed like hours, she stared as the slight glint of sunshine reflected on the frost-covered January ground. Snow spit through the air, blowing in waves. Finally, she spoke, "Never repeat the name."

"What name?"

"Swear it," she said, her voice trembling with emotion.

It was almost too much. I nodded.

"No. I need to hear you promise me. This name can never be spoken aloud."

"I swear," I said.

"Sparrow, Alleister Sparrow. He's currently in charge, but one day it will be his son, Sterling."

I wished for a pen to write the names down; however, from the way they sent a chill down my spine, I was most certain that I'd never forget.

～

The twisted and intriguing storytelling that you loved in Consequences and Infidelity is coming back at you with an all-new alpha anti-hero in the dark romance series Web of Sin, by New York Times bestselling author Aleatha Romig.

Preorder SECRETS, book one of the Web of Sin trilogy by Aleatha Romig ,today by tapping on the title.

THE END

Did you know that Paul and Jenn were referred to Dr. Kizer by the characters in UNCONVENTIONAL? If you enjoyed UNEXPECTED, please download UNCONVENTIONAL today and learn Dr. Kizer's secret of success... explore those desires!

WHAT TO DO NOW

LEND IT: Did you enjoy Unexpected? Do you have a friend who'd enjoy Unexpected? Unexpected may be lent one time. Sharing is caring!

RECOMMEND IT: Do you have multiple friends who'd enjoy my fun, erotic novellas? Tell them about it! Call, text, post, tweet...your recommendation is the nicest gift you can give to an author!

REVIEW IT: Tell the world. Please go to the retailer where you purchased this book, as well as Goodreads, and write a review. Please share your thoughts about Unexpected on:

*Amazon, *UNEXPECTED* Customer Reviews

*Barnes & Noble, *UNEXPECTED,* Customer Reviews

*iBooks, *UNEXPECTED* Customer Reviews

*Goodreads.com/Aleatha Romig

MORE FROM ALEATHA:

I hope you enjoyed my lighter side with a darker twist in UNEXPECTED. For more of my works ranging from dark to light check out these links:

THE VAULT NOVELLAS: (short, erotic reads exploring hidden fantasies)
UNCONVENTIONAL
UNEXPECTED
https://www.aleatharomig.com/the-vault-unconventional

THE CONSEQUENCES SERIES: (bestselling dark romance)
(First in the series FREE)
CONSEQUENCES
TRUTH

CONVICTED
REVEALED
BEYOND THE CONSQUENCES
BEHIND HIS EYES CONSEQUENCES
BEHIND HIS EYES TRUTH
RIPPLES (A Consequences stand-alone novel)
https://www.aleatharomig.com/consequences-series

THE INFIDELITY SERIES: (acclaimed romantic saga)
(First in the series FREE)
BETRAYAL
CUNNING
DECEPTION
ENTRAPMENT
FIDELITY
RESPECT (An Infidelity stand-alone novel)
https://www.aleatharomig.com/infidelity-series

INSIDIOUS (stand-alone smart, sexy thriller):
https://www.aleatharomig.com/insidious

THE LIGHT DUET: (romantic thriller duet)

INTO THE LIGHT
AWAY FROM THE DARK
https://www.aleatharomig.com/light-series

ALEATHA'S LIGHTER ONES (stand-alone light, fun, and sexy romances guaranteed to leave you with a smile and maybe a tear)
PLUS ONE
A SECRET ONE
ANOTHER ONE
ONE NIGHT
https://www.aleatharomig.com/light-series

ABOUT THE AUTHOR

Aleatha Romig is a New York Times, Wall Street Journal, and USA Today bestselling author who lives in Indiana, USA. She has raised three children with her high school sweetheart and husband of over thirty years. Before she became a full-time author, she worked days as a dental hygienist and spent her nights writing. Now, when she's not imagining mind-blowing twists and turns, she likes to spend her time with her family and friends. Her other pastimes include reading and creating heroes/anti-heroes who haunt your dreams!

Aleatha impresses with her versatility in writing. She released her first novel, CONSEQUENCES, in August of 2011. CONSEQUENCES, a dark romance, became a bestselling series with five novels and two companions released from 2011 through 2015. The compelling and epic story of Anthony and Claire Rawlings has graced more than half a million e-readers. Her first stand-alone smart, sexy thriller INSIDIOUS was next. Then Aleatha released the five-novel INFIDELITY series, a romantic suspense saga, that took the reading world by storm, the final book landing on three of the top bestseller lists. She ventured into traditional publishing with Thomas and Mercer. Her books INTO THE LIGHT and AWAY FROM THE DARK were published through this mystery/thriller publisher in 2016. In the spring of 2017, Aleatha again ventured into a different genre with her first fun and sexy stand-alone romantic comedy with the USA Today bestseller PLUS ONE.

Aleatha is a "Published Author's Network" member of the Romance Writers of America and PEN America. She is represented by Kevan Lyon of Marsal Lyon Literary Agency.

54961907R00084

Made in the USA
Middletown, DE
14 July 2019